From a Crooked Rib

NURUDDIN FARAH

Introduction by Richard Dowden

PENGUIN BOOKS

PENGUIN BOOKS

Published by the Penguin Group
Penguin Books Ltd, 80 Strand, London WC2R ORL, England
Penguin Putnam Inc., 375 Hudson Street, New York, New York 10014, USA
Penguin Books Australia Ltd, 250 Camberwell Road, Camberwell, Victoria 3124, Australia
Penguin Books Canada Ltd, 10 Alcorn Avenue, Toronto, Ontario, Canada M4V 3B2
Penguin Books India (P) Ltd, 11 Community Centre, Panchsheel Park, New Delhi – 110 017, India
Penguin Books (NZ) Ltd, Cnr Rosedale and Airborne Roads, Albany, Auckland, New Zealand
Penguin Books (South Africa) (Pty) Ltd, 24 Sturdee Avenue, Rosebank 2196, South Africa

Penguin Books Ltd, Registered Offices: 80 Strand, London WC2R ORL, England

www.penguin.com

First published by Heinemann Educational Books 1970
Published in Penguin Books 2003
2

Copyright © Nuruddin Farah, 1970
Introduction copyright © Richard Dowden, 2003
All rights reserved

Printed and bound in Great Britain by Antony Rowe Ltd, Chippenham, Wiltshire

INTRODUCTION

One of Nuruddin Farah's

favourite sayings is 'Never trust a self-definer'. Unsurprisingly he is reluctant to describe himself too precisely, but his nation, Somalia, is one of the most clearly self-defined on earth. Somalis have created a monumental self-image of a proud nomadic warrior race that can take on the world and win. Despite the self-destructive wars of the last two decades, Somalis will tell you that there is no country better than Somalia and no greater nation in the world. Serial civil wars, the collapse of Somalia as a nation state, the dispersal of millions of Somalis throughout the world, have apparently not prompted any doubt of even self-examination.

Farah left Somalia as a very young man but in exile he devoted his life to examining that self-image and exposing its hypocrisy. In different ways his stories reveal the inhumanity that lurks beneath those supposedly traditional Somali ways. His writing subverts the icons of Somali society, undermining them with irony, battering them with shocking images and appalling tales.

He first declared his intentions with the publication of *From a Crooked Rib* in 1970. One might have expected a first novel from a budding African writer in a newly independent country to be upholding traditional ways and exhorting a return to traditional values. At that time Heinemann's African Writers Series, which published the book, was a collection of thinly disguised autobiographies by young Africans describing the tribulations of growing up under colonial rule. They proclaimed a return to African values suppressed by colonialism. Only a few, like Chinua Achebe in *A Man of the People* and Ayi Kwei Armah in *The Beautiful Ones Are Not Yet Born*, were already warning of the awfulness of Africa's new rulers. Nuruddin Farah did something no one else dreamed of doing; he savagely attacked the traditional values of his own people, not from a desire to modernise them but to expose them as anti-human and hypocritical.

Farah developed this theme through his novels culminating in *Secrets* published in 1998. The story turns on the unmentionable taboos of incest and homosexuality. In *From a Crooked Rib* Farah attacks the traditional role of Somali women. Difficult to appreciate thirty-five years on, this young western-educated male African novelist, writing in English, even makes the main character of his first novel an illiterate nomadic runaway woman.

It is the story of Ebla, a young orphaned woman in a poor nomadic group who flees from a forced marriage. She ends up in the city where she finds herself powerless and as dependent on distant male relatives as she was on her grandfather in the bush. A perfunctory marriage, that seems little more than an excuse for a young man to have sex with her, leads to an equally meaningless divorce and then another even more cynical marriage with an older man who wants a mistress. Having no one to support her in the city and needing money to survive she is on the brink of falling into prostitution. It painfully exposes the powerlessness of women in Somali society and the shallowness of the customary respect for them. The Somali proverb says that women come from Adam's crooked rib. If you try to straighten the rib, you will break it. Yet Ebla is not broken. She emerges not as a mere victim but as someone who fights back and, in the end, secures a kind of triumph. At a time when the status of women was not high on the agenda of most writers or anyone else in Africa, *From a Crooked Rib* was a dazzling spark.

Richard Dowden, 2003

For
Hawa & Adam Bihi
& Waveney Charles

Part One

'God created Woman from a crooked rib;
and any one who trieth to
straighten it, breaketh it.'

A Somali traditional proverb

PROLOGUE

He could only curse. That was all
he could do. Other than that, he could give advice, but now
he cursed.

He squatted on the ground. On the dirty ground, his
feather-weight body lay. He couldn't weigh more than sixty
pounds. He grasped a rosary very tightly. On close examin-
ation, one would think that he was seeking support from the
string. His arms were stretched forward and his buttocks
were resting on his heels. He had no shoes on. He was an old
man – about eighty, or even ninety. He could have been
even more than that, and he could possibly have been less.
At the time when he was born, nobody bothered about the
date of birth of a child. A child would be one year old, even
if his birthday fell on the last day of spring. Spring was what
counted. The three months of spring meant everything: for
human beings as well as for animals. Weddings were
arranged in spring; wars were undertaken; blessings of the
Saints were sought; tribal fights were either started or ended.
Spring, therefore, meant everything. It meant happiness; it
meant green pasture for the cattle; it meant a great quantity
of milk from the cattle, which also meant agricultural
prosperity for some. Spring was a semi-god.

The old man squinted to see who was coming towards
him. It was his grandson – the brother of Ebla, who had run
away or had eloped with a man, nobody knew for certain.
The young boy also squatted on the ground, rubbed his
hands on his uncovered lap, then let his hand go through his

dark, wavy, unwashed hair which was full of dandruff. He was about sixteen, but, being the only son of a family whose mother and father had both died long time ago, hard labour had aged him. He had a piece of cloth to cover his rough body – rough, because nothing protected it from the sun or the thorn-bushes which he walked over when herding the camels.

'She has gone away. We know that for certain,' the young boy said.

The old man kept silent: maybe he was meditating. The young boy looked sorrowfully down at the ground. The old man counted the beads of his rosary. There were ninety-nine of them, which represented the names of God. He was totally emaciated. His colleagues in this world had reported back to God a long time ago. The people in the area wondered if he would ever die. When spoken to, he would narrate in the minutest detail the story of the war between Sayyed Mohamed Abdulle Hassan, the Somali Warrior, and the British. He talked of it as if it were a duel between the Sayyed (the Sayyed only, mind you) and the British. The Sayyed did this. The Sayyed did that. The Sayyed killed Corfield. The Sayyed negotiated with that tribe, who were rebels. The Sayyed eradicated the rebels afterwards. He would recite to you almost all the poems of the Sayyed. That was the only thing which could revive his enthusiasm in his past life – otherwise, he had no feeling. He could not hate nor could he love anything or anybody any more. He had lost his sense of pride, even before his only son – the father of Ebla and the young boy – had passed away. He had exchanged his pride in life for silence – or reticence.

But now he could not keep silent. He was an old man, and his main duty was to give advice; to refer to the days before the others were born; to talk about the rainy season to come; to say what one should do and what one should not say; to

4

lecture on the worship of the Almighty, to whom, he, an old man, had devoted his life many years ago.

Although nobody cared what he thought, the old man had many things to say, to the middle-aged as well as to the youngsters. The latter group were not as attentive to his word as the former, maybe because the young blood in them made them vigorous and rebellious.

Ebla's sudden departure had killed many things in him, although he did not know why. He had witnessed women of her age running away from their families into the bosom of a man to get married. He had seen many such incidents. He had done it himself. Or rather his wife had done it for his sake. But what made it quite sinister was the fact that he had nobody else to look after him. He had loved her more than he loved anybody else – when he had the power to love. He loved her more than he loved his eyes. 'May the Lord take me away if Ebla dies before myself,' he had said several times before, in private and in public. And he really meant it. Her brother was indifferent towards him. 'But he is only a young man,' he thought. 'And it is possible that he will know what a grandfather is for, when he has grown up.'

The old man pursed his lips and became nervous. He shivered in spite of the heat and his soft flesh quivered as if beaten by the wind. He gripped the beads of the rosary tightly. '*Alhamdulillah. Istagfurullah. Subhanallah,*' he prayed. He repeated and repeated and repeated the words. They aged with him. He must have said them more than a hundred billion times. But they were on the tip of his tongue today, conveying no message, other than the vibration of his vocal chord and his breathing. He thought it over from the time he heard that Ebla had gone away; must he or mustn't he curse her? He again gripped the beads of the rosary. The string snapped under the old man's weak fingers and the beads ran away – and into the hot sand.

The young boy stooped to collect the beads for him. But the old man silently shook his head. He motioned to the young boy to go away.

The old man very softly and quietly said his curse. 'May the Lord disperse your plans, Ebla. May He make you the mother of many a bastard. May He give you hell on this earth as a reward.'

The boy ran away, and told two other old men about his grandfather. When they came, they found him lying on the ground. He could have been dead, he could have been alive; but no one went near him.

He was an old man, no doubt. And either could have been possible.

I

A dwelling. It was a dwelling,
like any other dwelling in the neighbourhood. Not in the least
different. The number of human beings in the encampment
was ten times less than that of the cattle. It was the dwelling
of a certain *Jes* (a unit of several families living together). It
seemed to be unique and, in a way, it was. Every place has
its unique features. And this place had more than one.

In the dark, the huts looked more or less like ant-hills,
maybe of an exaggerated size. The huts were made of wattle,
weaved into a mat-like thing with a cover on top. They were
supported by sticks, acting as pillars. Each had one door –
all of four feet high. It was a portable home, to be put on
the hump-back of a camel when the time came for moving to
a pastoral area farther up or down, to the east or the west. It
was the portable hut, unlike the stone house or mud hut in
a town.

The lives of these people depended upon that of their
herds. The lives of the herds also depended upon the
plentiness or the scarcity of green grass. But would one be
justified in saying that their existence depended upon green
pasture – directly or indirectly? Yes: life did depend on
green pastures.

Ebla was a member of this *Jes*. She had been on the move
with them from the time she was born. Her father and
mother had died when she was very young. In fact, she
couldn't remember vividly anything about them. She had
always been entrusted to the care of her grandfather, who

7

was himself an invalid, though not such a bad one as all that. He always got through to the people, and was very much respected. And his word was very much listened to.

For a woman, she was very tall, but this was not exceptional here. She stood six feet high. She would have been very beautiful, had it not been for the disproportion of her body. She could not read nor write her name. She only knew the Suras, which she read when saying her prayers. She learnt these by heart, hearing them repeated many times by various people. She thought about things and people in her own way, but always respected the old and the dead. Her mother and father meant more to her than anybody else, except her grandfather, who was responsible for her upbringing.

Ebla became disappointed with life many times – in people more than a dozen times. But these occasions were not grave: the circumstances were minor, at least in the way she approached them. To her, a refusal did not matter. Neither would a positive answer make her pleased. But acceptance of her opinions, both by her relations and her would-be husbands, did make her pleased. She thought of many things a woman of her background would never think of. Translated, Ebla roughly means 'Graceful' and she always wanted her actions to correspond with her name.

Ebla had been toying with the idea of leaving home for quite some time. However, she did not know whether this was to be a temporary change of air – in a town – or a permanent departure. She loved her grandfather, but maybe she mistook pity for love. Anyway, it was only when she thought of her grandfather that she felt the wringing of her heart and a quick impulse not to leave him.

Problems are created by people, Ebla thought, still lying on her mat in the hut. But there is no problem without a solution. Maybe it is good that I should stay to take care of my grandfather, to see to it that he dies peacefully and is buried peacefully. But should I think of someone who does not think of me? It is he who has given my hand to the old man, exchanging me for camels.

She let her hand touch the mat on which she had been lying awake the whole night. It was the same mat on which she sat to talk to many of her suitors, in the dark. In this same hut – or in another one: maybe in a different area, twenty or thirty miles farther up or down, in one direction or another. She sniggered at what some had said to her. She enjoyed talking to others. But none of them was an old man like Giumaleh, the one to whom fate had handed her over. It was yesterday morning that her grandfather had accepted Giumaleh's proposal. He was an old man of forty-eight: fit to be her father. Two of his sons had alternately courted her. But only the younger one was very keen on her. Probably he did not propose because his elder brother had not yet got married. At least, that was the hint that he gave – not to Ebla in person, but to friends. Gossip goes around swiftly: women hear a lot and talk a lot, and tell many lies. But Ebla did not believe a word of it. Obstinate, they would say, maybe hammering the word on her had made her that way. Maybe in a way she was obstinate.

She closed her eyes and imagined herself in the same bed with Giumaleh. Horrible. She just could not imagine it without going absolutely berserk. It was madly terrifying. The way things were, nobody seemed to care whether they harmed one another. Everybody for himself. No one gave a damn if something he did was inconvenient to others. One came out of one's mother's womb alone. One tried to solve one's problems alone. One died alone, isolated. One was put in a grave, and left behind under the ground. As soon as the corpse had been put in the grave and everyone had headed for his home to mourn, it was said that the dead heard the

9

sound of people. Even the sound which was made by their feet. That is what the prophet and great saints had said.

Soft warm air blew the door to and fro: very comforting. 'It makes one pleased,' she thought, 'the wind blowing things like that.' Actually what served as the door was a piece of cloth hanging from above the ceiling just to hide those inside. It would be inconvenient to be inside those huts with nothing to hide you.

Ebla stood up and dusted her robe, a very big robe wrapped around her body. A piece of it hung on her back, to serve as a baby-carrier or even as a vessel, or a shoulder-cover – or for countless other purposes.

She was very much worried, not for herself, but for her grandfather. She could not dismiss the thought just by shrugging her shoulders. She was not that type. She was a woman, a responsible woman of eighteen, going on nineteen.

Ordinarily, she was not a weak-minded girl. Not once in her life had she stopped doing anything because it would harm others. But this time, it was different. It was too much for her, far too much. She could not bear to think of waiting to get married to Giumaleh. To be in the doldrums – or to disappoint everyone, especially her grandfather? If she stayed, she thought, she would always be in low spirits. And if she went what would happen?

Yes. What if she went?

Something rang in her mind. But where would she go to? And to whom? And with whom?

Next to her, her friend, a girl of her own age, was snoring in her sleep. But she looked absolutely dead. Ebla stood up. Her left arm was asleep. She massaged it with her right hand. The edge of her robe lay underneath her friend's knee. Ebla tried to give it a tug without waking up her friend. At first she appeared to have woken up. Ebla stopped, motionless for a while. But the friend had put more of Ebla's robe underneath her body. Decidedly (and come what may, she thought) she pulled her robe. Thank God! The robe pulled out. And the friend still lay asleep, as if undisturbed.

Many hours of the night still remained. Ebla dreaded the long hours ahead of her, awaiting her as it in an ambush: an enemy, an unidentified enemy, who fixed his eyes on you when he felt like it. But she walked out into the warm night to think over the situation.

She wished she were not a woman. But would being a man make her situation any better? She wondered.

'But let me sort out my ideas; and see what I can do about them,' she told herself.

2

Escape! To get free from all
restraints, from being the wife of Giumaleh. To get away
from unpleasantries. To break the ropes society had wrapped
around her and to be free and be herself. Ebla thought of all
this, and much else.

'But why is a woman, a woman? To give companionship
to man? To beget him children? To do a woman's duty? But
that is only in the house. What else?' she asked herself.
'Surely a woman is indispensable to man, but do men realize
it?

'A man needs a woman. A woman needs a man. Not to the
same degree? A man needs a woman to cheat, to tell lies to,
to sleep with. In this way a baby is born, weak and forlorn.
He decides to belittle his mother immediately he is old
enough to walk. He slides away, becomes a heavy burden
until he is independent, gets his basic education, like
talking, walking, eating, under the care of his mother. When
a child, he fidgets about like a lid on top of a boiler. He is
infuriating at this stage – he should be put in a cage. After
a while, he walks, he talks – only his mother's language at
first. He smiles at his mother. . . . But Giumaleh is the
wrong match,' she suddenly told herself. 'I definitely can't
marry him.'

But who or what should she escape from? This was the
real question which needed to be answered. Inside her, she
knew why she wanted to escape. Actually it was more than
a want: it was a desire, a desire stronger than anything, a

thing to long for. Her escape meant her freedom. Her escape meant her new life. Her escape meant her parting with the country and its harsh life. Her escape meant the divine emancipation of the body and soul of a human being.

She desired, more than anything, to fly away; like a cock, which has unknotted itself from the string tying its leg to the wall. She wanted to fly away from the dependence on the seasons, the seasons which determine the life or death of the nomads. And she wanted to fly away from the squabbles over water, squabbles caused by the lack of water, which meant that the season was bad. She wanted to go away from the duty of women. Not that she was intending to feel idle and do nothing, nor did she feel irresponsible, but a woman's duty meant loading and unloading camels and donkeys after the destination had been reached, and that life was routine: goats for girls and camels for boys got on her nerves more than she could stand. To her, this allotment of assignments denoted the status of a woman, that she was lower in status than a man, and that she was weak. 'But it is only because camels are stupid beasts that boys can manage to handle them,' she always consoled herself. She loathed this discrimination between the sexes: the idea that boys lift up the prestige of the family and keep the family's name alive. Even a moron-male cost twice as much as two women in terms of blood-compensation. As many as twenty or thirty camels are allotted to each son. The women, however, have to wait until their fates give them a new status in life: the status of marriage. A she-camel is given to the son, as people say 'tied to his navel' as soon as he is born. 'Maybe God prefers men to women,' she told herself.

But Ebla had no answers to the questions how to escape, where should she escape to, whom should she go to, and when she should escape.

To escape. To be free. To be free. To be free. To escape. These were inter-related.

How to escape? Where to escape to?

Throughout the night, she had been thinking of the easiest method by which she could escape without her grandfather and her brother and the others knowing about it. Her future husband had gone away to the next dwelling, and would be back on the morrow, she had learnt the previous evening. But how? How to escape? She thought about the matter seriously, but there seemed to be no way out. The way to escape was not clear to her. Gradually the clues dripped into her mind as the spring rain drips on to the green grass with the morning dawn. Things came to light. Situations became more friendly. She knew what she should do: escape alone and join the caravan going to Belet Wene, which would leave after a while, she told herself. 'After a while,' she repeated to herself, 'After a while.'

There was always plenty of time in the country. One spoke of morning, when one should say one's prayers, or wake up to attend to the wants of the beasts. One spoke of 'harr' when the beasts would be put out to graze: the young men then went out and sat under the shade of a tree to play cards, and the old men talked poetry and told proverbs, while the women sat apart, talking together while they mended mats or while the older women plaited the hair of their young unmarried daughters. Everybody had a certain duty to keep him or her busy. Even the young boys had games to play, throwing sticks after each other, go-run-'n'-catch the opponent, jumping races, and much else. This was life which took place within sight of the settlement of the central family. The central family consisted of women, children, the invalid, goats and a few camels to provide them with milk. Young men took care of the camels and moved around on their own, but occasionally called upon the central family, with the camels.

Ebla had learnt, even before she had seriously decided to fly away, that the only reasonable place she could go to would be a town. She was not sure which town would suit her best. Which place would give her all the things she wanted?

Outside, the morning was lonely as if it were a widow whose second husband had just died and who intended never to re-marry but to face hardship and loneliness. The wind was sad as if it were a poor student whose ink-bottle had just broken into pieces and whose ink had coloured the ungrateful ground. The trees were standing apart as if they were afraid of each other and as if they would contaminate each other had they shaken and touched. Silence was the only refuge they all knew. That was the only language they could comprehend. The morning did not expect to be followed by another morning and another morning and another morning. The wind was glad to be sad for a change, maybe just as the student would be glad at breaking the bottle of ink to give him a legitimate excuse to stay outside the school premises. The trees were delighted to stay apart lest they should multiply and quarrel over space.

Ebla had reached a decision in the meantime. She murmured to herself something she herself did not quite understand.

'Destiny and fate can be worked out,' she told herself. 'One dies only once, and only when one's Time comes. Nobody knows when Time will knock on his door. And when It does, It will be welcome. But until tomorrow, let me try to tackle my problem. Maybe Death will escort the morning.'

3

The work of the previous day had
given her a hang-over. She realized this only when she was
about to make the move. 'A hard day's work has always left
an after-effect on me, so why should I worry,' she told
herself.

The clock would strike four in the morning. It was
Tuesday – to her like any other day, for even Friday was not
different. To men perhaps it was, as they all went to a pray-
ing-place, or to a mosque. To women Friday only meant
more work, more washing and more cooking to be done.

She had nothing to carry along with her. She never
owned much, only a spare sheet to wear when the one she
had on got dirty – and it was old. The muezzin had not
announced the nearing of the morning prayers: the first
wailing had not been heard. The sound of watering camels
had not yet started. She stopped as if to take something,
but it was only to ease up the hang-over. She touched her
toes and heard the sound her joints made. The hut was very
dark. There were no matches to light, no maps to take. The
only fire which provided a dim light had been blown out
before Ebla and her friend had fallen asleep. Ebla's colleague
was still snoring her head off. Ebla stretched her long arms
down to pick up her shoes and the sheet. She had placed
them somewhere in the evening. She took both of them in
her hands and walked out of the hut. She put one foot outside and one inside and kept standing there motionless. For
a while she hesitated, not wondering whether or not she

should go – she had settled that and there was nothing to make her change her mind – but should she or shouldn't she tell her colleague in the hut where she intended to go?

She lifted her foot back. Her body stood an inch away from the door. She could feel the mild wind. She turned her back on the door and headed inwards. She stopped a few inches from where her friend lay snoring. She wanted to call to her friend and say that she had decided to escape. She opened her mouth, but before she was able to say anything, she heard a bang on the outside wall. She stopped, wanting to find out what had made the noise, to see if anybody was outside, and to regain her lost self, for she did not know for a fraction of a second who she was. The noise had not been repeated and Ebla was prepared to go out and not wake up her colleague. 'It is much better that way,' she thought to herself.

She swayed as if she were drunk.

The whole area was silent. Not a sound was to be heard. The unmarried males slept outside the huts and in the clearing. White sheets covered their bodies. Ebla passed near them, not making any sound. She walked bare-footed, and wrapped her sheet around her shoes, and put the bundle between her arm and ribs. She tiptoed as if she were a thief who had preyed upon somebody whom he knows. She cast her eyes downward. She finally reached the entrance to the dwelling. It was a thorn-fence, which had just been built. There was a stick put across, which served as the gate. Should she go underneath or should she lift the stick? She stopped and bent down to see if she could pass underneath. Being unable to do that she lifted the stick. The gate creaked. The prickles stood out and the stick had touched some of them as she lifted it. Her heart began pounding frightfully fast. She thought she had made a loud noise. She looked around, but there was nothing coming, nobody, not a living soul. The cock crowed, then there was silence again, She replaced the stick in a hurry and stood on the outside of the dwelling-boundary.

'My God, I am out,' she said to herself.

She headed west and in the direction where the travellers to Belet Wene would pass by. She hid herself under a big tree, near the detour, which encircled the main road.

'*Alhamdulillah, Subhanallah, Istagfurullah.*' She kept on repeating these words, which did not convey much to a young woman of her background. She said them because she had heard others say them. She knew the words were Arabic and that they were God's words, and sacred. She counted on her finger-joints just as she had seen others do it. Actually, she let her thumbs run over her fingers one by one. Thus rhythmically, and sometimes inaccurately, she counted, saying each word three times, until she had said every word ninety-nine times: that was the number which represented God's names.

Fate in her faith. Ebla put her faith and her fate along with it into the hands of God. 'And I am certain that God will understand my situation. And of course, He won't let me down.

'If I am asked by the caravan people where I am going, what shall I say? I suppose I must tell them the truth. But what is truth – that which corresponds to the notions we have in mind or that which corresponds to our doings? Why do we think differently from the way we behave? If I tell the truth, then it won't get me anywhere, for certain. If I say I ran away because my grandfather had decided to give my hand in (sacred?) marriage to a man – an old man, I must say to drive home the point that I had to escape. But what is wrong in getting married to a man – old or young? Age doesn't determine the genuineness of marriage, does it? Sometimes there are old men who are much more likeable husbands than young ones. People are argumentative, and surely they will bring up this question.

' "You are allowed to tell lies if the situation makes it necessary," said Prophet Mohammed. That is what our Prophet has said, and everything he said ought to be obeyed. But is this a necessity – I mean telling lies under the present circumstances? Every situation has its serious side – is this the most serious situation or are there many more to follow it?'

Ebla had not been able to reach a decision when she heard the caravans approaching her. Things appeared to crowd in upon her instantly.

The travellers could see her tall figure – and it gave more charm to the light caused by the dawn. Ebla was nature, nature had become personified in her. The trees, the earth, the noise, the talking of the caravan people were also part of nature. The dawn-wind caressed her cheeks. The birds chirped their songs. The stars withdrew into their tiny holes in the sky – maybe to rest and at the same time to get charged for the night which would await them. The moon faded into the blue colour of the sky – and lost its conspicuousness. Silence. Death of voices. Feet-shufflings. The still unused energy in the peasants of whom the caravan was made up was shown in their powerful strides – each of them a separate individual. The milk which they had drunk before they started their trip shook inside their bellies. The camels walked haughtily as if whatever they carried on their backs was their own and as if the peasants who walked behind them, with sticks in their hands, were there to guard the property. The master mistook himself for the slave. Heaps upon heaps of cow-hide, goat-hide, frankincense and other articles for sale unknowingly danced their way to their altar in the town.

As if he wasn't sure of what he had seen, the young man

who led the first camel by the reins, opened his eyes a little bit more. His hesitations confirmed, he said: 'What are you doing here, cousin Ebla?'

Although she wasn't his cousin, in that area people still address each other in those terms – that is their polite form of saying hello even to a stranger.

'I am sick,' Ebla said, thinking that would explain everything.

'What are you doing here? And especially if you are sick? Home is a long way from here,' said the young man, as tall as Ebla. By now, he had forgotten that he was leading the caravan. The first camel had mischievously led the rest of the camels astray. The young man, therefore, had to stride away from her to resume his responsibility. The other people in the caravan had by then come level with her. One by one, they asked her about her mission to town.

She told them why she was there: 'I am sick, I need some injections. And I want to buy some clothes.'

'For your wedding?' some had asked.

'Yes,' she said and nodded her head.

And she smiled ironically.

Part Two

'There's a man all over for you,
blaming on his boots
the faults of his feet.'

Samuel Beckett: *Waiting for Godot*

4

At the outskirts of the town, she
could hear the hideous noise so common in Belet Wene, the
smoke which could have smothered anybody, the peasants
coming out of town after they had bought and sold what they
wanted, and the young boys playing football, with a ball
which was made out of pieces of worn-out clothes stitched
together. Before she knew what was happening or where she
was, she was somewhere near the bazaar.

Ebla stopped for a while to look closely at the townspeople. Inwardly she was annoyed, perhaps because nobody
had noticed her aloofness or perhaps because she could not
see anybody whom she knew. (But she had not known more
than a hundred persons in her life; and perhaps, she never
wanted to know more.) Her colleagues from the caravan had
gone ahead. It was only when somebody called to her that
she came back to her senses and woke up. Then she found
nobody but herself, dressed in the long wide robe, which
stretched out in all directions, down to the ground, to the
sides, ruffling in the wind. She looked at her robe as she
walked, lifting between her thumb and forefinger the corners
which touched the ground. The wind blew on to her belly.
Her right side was naked and one voluptuous breast could be
seen, nodding, saying 'hello' to the robe which caressed it.
Ebla thought that the clothes worn by the townspeople were
indecent. 'But maybe I am wrong – let me get closer,' she
told herself, 'and see how they dress exactly. Tomorrow; I
will be able to pass judgement tomorrow, perhaps.'

It was the first time she had ever been in a town. Once they were about three hundred miles from Kallafo. The family wanted to go there to sell some camels, but it was not possible. Some inter-tribal warfare had broken out and had prevented them making their trip.

Ebla had never believed what people said about towns. She had listened to many of them describe towns: Kallafo, Galcaio, Baidoa, Warder, Hargeisa had all been described to her by different people and at different times, when she was in different moods. Some of them liked the towns they had talked about, others hated them. But it all came to one thing: that people's tastes differ. She must find out something for herself, she told herself. She had her spare robe in her hands, even though it was stained in parts by the sweat from her palms: even so, it was tolerably clean and wearable.

She had queried people about her cousin and his wife, whether or not they were nice. She was very pleased to hear that they were and that they were in need of a maid-servant. The wife was pregnant and she needed a hand; Ebla felt that she could help.

'But this is Belet Wene,' she thought. 'Oh, my Lord, what a large town!'

It was about one in the afternoon. The market-place was not very busy. Papers, turned yellow because of age, flew about and along the roads. It appeared to Ebla as if they had been intentionally scattered. To her, this was one of the phenomena of a town. The sun was very hot, maybe hotter than it was in the country; or perhaps the town's sun came nearer to the earth than that in the country, she thought. The clouds moved in the sky, first heading in one direction then in the opposite. From a very narrow road, some children came out running. Two of them were stark naked: the kids played as if they cared for nothing in the universe.

'But a town is more than a dwelling of a clan,' she thought

to herself. There were far more people than she had imagined. She looked around. She saw huts and houses and
buildings unlike the ones she had been accustomed to. The
circular huts were miraculously beautiful from outside. A
car hooted from nearby: she wondered what it could be and
how it could move along all by itself, without anybody
pulling or pushing it. 'It is the magic of the white man,'
someone nearby voluntarily explained to her. She left it at
that.

Now they were going below the arched building of
Belet Amin, the town of peace, constructed by the Sayyid,
the warrior about whom she had heard so much. She stopped
to touch the arch herself. It was something very novel to
her: she had never seen anything like it. Her grandfather
would have rejoiced to see this. Several times, he had tried to
give her some hints of town life, but it had been no use; she
had not believed a word of what he had said. She was
obstinate – or so it seemed.

Now that they had come to the centre of the town,
nobody from the group offered to escort her to her cousin's
place. This cousin was thrice removed, but that hardly
mattered. His wife needed a maid-servant and naturally she
wanted to give a hand. At first she would tell him, just as she
had told her fellow-travellers, that she had come to town for
a medical check-up. That would sound a legitimate reason
to stay with them for a week or so in case her service was not
needed.

How would she be able to help? She knew quite well that
town life was different from the life she had led. Perhaps she
should be more submissive than she had been to others and
in that way she might learn much and be of assistance to
others.

A young man was singled out from the group to take
her to her cousin's place. He gave her a sign to follow him.

She had already been keeping her spare robe and that was all she owned. She tucked the robe underneath her arm. Nobody wished her good luck or anything like that, because they did not have the slightest idea what her intentions were.

The young man slowed down to keep pace with her and to have a close look at her – not exactly at her, but at a part of her. The wind now had started to blow hard and Ebla's naked ribs showed more. She could feel the breeze fondling her belly; and the young man threw a sideways glance at the naked spot. He went on as before, not showing the slightest desire, at least not externally. Ebla walked vigorously at his side, throbbing. Blessing whom? Scared of whom? And of what? Wishing what? Praying probably to God. She was silent, her hands going to and fro, her robe stretching out to the sides like the wings of a plane. Before they reached her cousin's house, she saw the young man's severe eyes. She lowered her eyes coyly and re-tightened the robe, covering her breast.

Ebla and the young man found themselves at the door of her cousin's house. The young man said that he would go back to the group, and that she should do things for herself. He left her. She did not thank him.

5

She was alone. The man had left

her. She knew why the young man had left her: the townspeople never liked anyone who brought them guests from
the country. Ebla felt unspeakable agony when she realized
that she would have to do everything for herself. For the first
time in her life she faced the problem of getting something
done with no assistance. This was particularly difficult on
her first day in a town, where the devils lived along with the
saints, and whores face to face with their relations. 'But this
time I shall have to cope,' she encouraged herself. 'It is
absolutely necessary.'

She walked on a few steps and into the house. A cow was
tied by the leg to the wall; a calf, probably the cow's, could
also be seen elsewhere in the other direction. The cow ate its
green grass, and mooed. Ebla felt more at home being near
the cow than she would with the townspeople, she guessed.
A goat bleated from within a small hut to her right. 'Oh,
marvellous,' she told herself. 'I only wish we had a camel
around.' She looked in the direction of the cow and went
towards it. The beast could not reach the grass that it had
unintentionally pushed away with its tongue. It dug its feet
into the ground as it knelt down on its hind legs, then put
out its tongue to pull the grass so that it could eat. But
instead of coming nearer, the grass went farther away,
farther and farther. Ebla walked over and pushed the grass
nearer and nearer. The cow at last got hold of a bundle and
bit into it, hard and properly.

Ebla gave a happy smile. 'Good,' she said to herself. Then the calf bleated. 'Maybe it's hungry too,' she speculated. She looked towards the calf and could not see any grass near it. So, placing her spare robe on the ground, she picked up a handful of grass and headed towards the calf. She placed it just under the nose of the beast, and walked away feeling contented.

All this time, Gheddi had been looking at what she was doing, but could not understand what she was after. He looked at her from behind the window, so that she would not be able to see him, even if she looked. He talked to someone inside the room and then came out.

'*Nabad*,' Ebla heard a man's voice from behind. She had just placed the grass in front of the calf.

Ebla turned around, her eyes downcast, her heart beating faster and faster. The strange man came nearer, and the nearer he came, the stranger he appeared to her. She wanted to get away before he appropriated her, but she was slow. He looked at her as if he knew her. Her eyes were still lowered, her hands dangling, as helpless as a man drowning. Her feet felt very heavy, as if they could not support the rest of her body.

He repeated '*Nabad*', which means 'peace be unto you'.

She looked around. She thought that he had spoken to somebody else, but she could not see anybody else.

She looked at him. He was approximately thirty-five and had a full beard painted with henna, but he was shorter than the men from her dwellings.

All that Ebla wanted to do was go away and disappear – run, run away. And she would have run away had he not stopped her.

'But just wait,' he said. She waited. She could hear his footsteps coming nearer. The order he had given to her resounded in her ears. She was amazed because of the gentleness of his voice.

'Who do you want to see?' he asked her.

'Someone,' she replied in a low voice, which he could hardly hear.

'Are you looking for a particular person?' She glanced at him, not understanding.

'I mean in this house. Or even in the neighbourhood?'

'Yes,' she said.

'Then who is it?'

'My cousin.'

'Your cousin? Here in town?'

'Yes,' she said.

'What is his name?' Ebla kept silent.

'I might know where he lives.'

'They say he lives here.'

'In this house?' She nodded. She wished she had never come to the town.

'I am the owner of this house.'

'The name of my cousin is Gheddi,' she said, not knowing that it was to him that she was speaking.

'My name is Gheddi.'

Gheddi stood motionless for a while. He could not work out who this girl was. And, anyway, these country people always claimed to be the cousin of someone or other. He immediately remembered a young man who had come to him and said that he was a cousin of his (ten times removed) and before he had known what he was doing, Gheddi gave him a place to sleep and something to eat. The young man stole some clothes and twenty shillings and had never been seen again. But this was a girl. 'She would not come to steal, would she?' he asked himself.

'What is your name?'

'My name is Ebla.'

'And what is the name of your father?' She told him. He pitied her. He knew the situation under which she had grown up, that she was a motherless child, and afterwards had also lost her father.

'Come on in,' he said. 'Don't stand in the sun. You must be tired.'

She turned around and went to collect her sheet from where she had left it when she went to feed the beasts.

Gheddi led her to the interior of the wattle-mud hut. Inside it was not as spacious as it looked from outside. There were two beds, on one of which a woman was lying, with her eyes half closed. Also there were a number of nails on the wall which served as hangers, and a few boxes on the dung-floor. She twisted her head and mumbled something to herself, biting her lips.

Ebla stood in the doorway to have a closer look. Gheddi came over to where his wife lay. He placed his hand on the edge of the bed. He had his back turned to Ebla, but she could feel that he communicated with the woman, just by touching her on the shoulders, as if consoling her, telling her not to worry about the pain she was feeling or about the wishes she had had. He now faced Ebla again, and said:

'Come on in. Why should you stand there like a stranger? Come inside.' Ebla obeyed.

'This is my wife,' he said, pointing at the woman lying on the bed, whose figure was still vague as far as Ebla was concerned. 'She is pregnant,' she told herself. Neither of the women said a word. 'I will be on my way to the shop. In another minute or two I will be gone. You are tired. You can sleep for a while,' he said to Ebla. To his wife he said, 'This is Ebla, my cousin. There you are.'

After saying this, he left and the two women were all alone. They could perhaps talk to each other like women, Gheddi must have thought.

6

Gheddi's wife turned in the bed.

Her belly would have prevented her sitting upright had she
tried to. Nine months' pregnancy – she felt pain, especially in
the back: the spinal cord seemed to make things worse. Her
legs served her no more, her hands seemed to be there only
to wipe away the moisture that had been the result of the
heat. Some drips of perspiration, sour in taste but queer and
good for a pregnant woman like herself, dropped into her
mouth, or into her eyes, the latter being absolutely unbearable. The cloth covered down to her knees. The heat
was intolerable. Her shoulders were bare. A head-scarf also
covered her long hair. Now that she sat up, the cloth went
upwards exposing part of her once lovely, but now weak
thighs. There was no male in the room and Ebla was no
longer a stranger. It did not matter whether her thighs were
covered or uncovered.

'Ebla, is this the first time you have ever come to this
town, or did you come before?' she whispered.

'This is my first visit,' Ebla replied.

'And when will you go back?' Ebla thought how hard it
must be for her to talk. She wanted to say that she had no
intention to go back, but she hesitated.

'I don't know.' They both kept silent. In the meanwhile,
they heard the mooing of a cow, followed by the bleating of
its calf. This was followed by the other cows, which had
just come back from the grazing ground outside town.

'It is not time for these cows to come back. The bastard

cowherd doesn't keep them at the· grazing fields, even if there is lots for them to eat,' Gheddi's wife complained.

Ebla got up from the place where she had seated herself, and said: 'I shall go and put the cows in the cots.'

'Yes, do that,' said Gheddi's wife. Ebla, still tired from the tedious trip and still in her once white robe which by now had changed to a brownish colour because of the dust, walked away.

'And tie them by the legs to the poles in the cot. Otherwise they will go to the calves and the calves will suck them dry.' Ebla went out convincing herself that the life in a town did not resemble that of the country. She thought in these terms when she headed towards the cows.

She ran to and fro, trying to keep the cows from the calves. Twice she had to curse a calf-less cow. Later, she learnt that it was a rebel cow. It refused to be tied by the leg to the pole and before that it also did not want to be dragged into the cot. Ebla thought that the other cows had every reason to object to being tied to the poles, but this cow had no calf to run to. As is usual, the calf had been killed and eaten only five days after it was born. The cow had given birth for the first time and this was done to teach it that, in case its future calf died, it could be milked with ease.

Cows are beasts, calves are beasts and so are goats. 'But we are beasts, too,' she thought. 'Isn't my grandfather a beast? If one shows one's bestiality by what one does then we are only better than these beasts by trying to explain our doings in such a way that we won't appear ridiculous to our friends.

'Kill a beast's calf,' she continued thinking. 'And to him it is as painful as it is to human beings. But if this is not brought to an end, one day the strain will make them speak out, blast everybody and reveal their anguish which they have been storing up for so long. Sayyed Mohammed loved one of his beasts, the horse he called *Hhin Fineen*, more than his sons. He never composed a line of poetry in his sons' praise, but he composed many poems in praise of his beast. I like the Sayyed, because he loved his beasts. But I dislike him because he murdered many people for no reason.'

Although Ebla hated laying about animals, she had to do so when the cows objected to being tied to the poles. After she had tied up all the cows, she came back to where Gheddi's wife, Aowralla, lay on the bed. As Ebla came in, she woke up with a smile, showing her teeth. She very cautiously turned herself over in bed; Ebla felt a bit uneasy watching her do this.

'How are they?' Aowralla asked Ebla.

'Fine. All healthy and fat. But there is one nasty cow. He did not want to be tied on to anything and with anything.'

'I know.'

'What is his name?' (In Somali, a cow is spoken of as he and not she or it.)

'Whose?' Aowralla asked.

'The cow's.'

'Bafto.' The name means white, and the cow was white.

'It is very beautiful, otherwise.'

'Yes, it is,' affirmed Aowralla. 'But we nickname him "Toje" – he is a rebel. Imagine me milking him in this condition.'

'Do you really do that?'

'Yes. I did it this morning. He kicked me here.' She touched her ribs. 'It aches, it has been aching all day, but I am better now. I feel much better.'

Aowralla turned over on to the other side, thus turning her back on Ebla. Ebla stood with her hands resting on her ribs and her elbows stretched out. Then she staggered to the bed to rest, to lie for a while, to relax, as her cousin had said. The bed was more than kneehigh. She touched it in the middle. She felt that something was moving, bouncing, hitting back, jumping up high into the air. The mattress reacted to her touches, the bed was springy. Ebla turned around.

She straightened herself. Her breasts slightly protruding, her legs quivering with tiredness, her eyes half closed with slumber, her breath increasing, Ebla moved backwards. She touched the cold edge with her buttocks. 'Good. The whole bed is not jumpy,' she realized. Her hand preceded her. She closed her eyes again, and felt herself in a wonderland. She lifted her body, and jumped, jumped up on to the middle of the bed: one high jump, then it was all right. This was only followed by little tiny bounces, which she enjoyed. She removed her shoes, flung them down, and then succumbed to drowsiness.

She breathed hard, and found that the bed was comfortable, not as terrible as she had previously imagined. Once she stretched herself on the bed, she knew she would fall asleep. She was drowsy, but, as she was falling asleep, she heard Aowralla calling to her:

'Ebla.'

'Yes?'

She was *en route* for happiness and relaxation and hated someone calling her at that particular moment.

'Ebla.'

'Yes, what is it?' she said, as she sat up in the bed, eyes half closed and voice unclear.

'Come,' said Aowralla.

'All right,' she replied. She came down and walked up to where Aowralla lay on the other bed. She was bare-footed, and she felt the blisters on her right foot.

'What is it?'

'I want water,' replied Aowralla, caressing the belly with her left hand and putting her right hand underneath her head to serve as a pillow.

Ebla could not hear her clearly, Aowralla had to say it a

few times, and it was only when Ebla lowered her head to listen that she understood what Aowralla wanted.

'I will get you water,' she said aloud as if speaking to a deaf person.

'But where from?' she asked herself. She went round and round at random and finally found where the clay water-pot was. She drank a glass of water herself, and then brought one to Aowralla.

It was five-thirty in the afternoon.

Ebla walked away with an empty glass in her hand. In fact, she hobbled away, scarcely placing her right foot on the floor. She had blisters on her right foot. She laid the glass on the table and returned to Aowralla who was moaning and groaning.

Aowralla opened her mouth to say something.

After much effort, Aowralla was able to get through to her, 'Go and milk the cows,' she said. 'But don't milk them dry, except the calf-less one, which yields more milk.'

Ebla ran back and forth trying to find out where the milk containers, the milk receptacles and the string to tie the cows' legs were. She once had the desire to go to Aowralla and say that she would run back to her grandfather who needed her help just as much, or even more, and to whom she owed her own existence. 'But she is pregnant,' she thought.

The cows mooed, the calves bleated, wishing that she would give them grass, as Aowralla used to at this time of the evening, before they were milked. But the grass had not been brought, as their mistress had not got out of bed for the whole day.

'A hungry beast is far more pitiable than we imagine,' thought Ebla. 'But who understands beasts?' She was actually more in harmony with them, now that they were near to her, and she wished she could help them.

'But what can I do? I am new here, and I don't know where exactly one gets grass for the beasts. I have seen the outskirts of the town but, apart from that section, the place is full of buildings. Why do they build houses everywhere? Houses! Mud-houses, stone houses, houses of dung, houses of nothing but sticks. Growing grass around the area would be much more beneficial to everyone. Our lives are not more precious than those of the beasts, and I wonder if we don't need them more than they need us? What do they get from us? Nothing.'

It was strange how she had become obsessed by the situation the beasts were in. 'They cannot find their way out,' she thought.

She was standing outside now, brooding over what she should do. Aowralla's groaning did not matter to her as much as the cows' hunger: mooing struck her as pathetic, intolerable and worth attending to.

Aowralla lay in bed, and inside her the baby rang the bell to come out. The midwife had not come. But how could she anyway, when nobody had called her?

Cows mooed. Calves bleated. Aowralla groaned. Ebla hesitated. 'What should I do? Who should I take care of first? Aowralla is an acquaintance since this afternoon, although she is my cousin's wife. The beasts have been with me from the day I opened my eyes on the world.' Still the cows mooed and the calves bleated. Still Aowralla groaned, but her groaning had become graver than ever. Ebla had decided; no longer was she hesitant about attending those with whom she felt more in harmony.

She walked towards the cows. Her hands were empty, but her heart was full of sympathy for them. 'I will explain to everybody later,' she told herself. 'I will ask forgiveness from my cousin and naturally he will give it. Aowralla is not conscious about what is going on around her. But how can I ask the beasts to excuse me if I don't attend to them? I know I am just as much a beast as they are. They eat, sleep and moo; they don't care a straw what goes on around them – they don't preoccupy themselves. How lucky they are! Maybe they don't know, maybe they do. But it is we humans who don't understand them.'

She stood beside one of them. It mooed loudly and lifted its head to sniff at Ebla's hand, which she had stretched forward. It sniffed at it, and then mooed again as if Ebla's hand stank from something dreadfully bad. Ebla was offended and hit the cow by the horn with her hand. Obediently the cow lowered its head. Ebla felt pain in her wrist. She hit the horn again, then nursed her hand with the other one. 'But I deserve it,' she thought. 'Why should I hit it? It has not done me or anyone any harm. It is only a misunderstanding between us.'

Now that her right hand ached, she stretched out her left one. She wanted to befriend the cow. It licked her hand.

'You and I are friends, aren't we?' She spoke to the beast, caressing the nape of its neck. The cow lifted its head as if giving a nod. Ebla felt quite happy. She went round the cot, calling on each of the beasts. Although they weren't as responsive or even aggressive as the first cow, she felt happier than she had been since she came to Belet Wene.

Ebla heard the groaning of Aowralla, which had worsened. She ran into the room. Aowralla turned over and over – not actually turned over, but moved her lower part. Her robe had fallen out one side, and she was naked – stark naked, except for a small part that hung from her nape.

Ebla stood helpless. Aowralla's legs instinctively fell apart. Ebla, recalling the operation that she had heard about that was done on other women, looked around for what could help her as instruments for the operation.

After a quarter of an hour, a baby cried in the room. Very softly and quietly Ebla prayed to God, the Almighty, 'Oh my Lord,' she reasoned with Him, 'If You think I should stay on here, although I feel quite strange and rejected at the same time, then say it. Say it in the form of any action. Make me do things. Let Your blessings run through my blood, be in my food, be ahead of me, and at my back too. But if You have deprived me of the best qualities and denied me the authority to do things my own way, why not deprive me of this life? It is nothing but a loan, and the longer a loan is not settled, the worse it is for the one who has borrowed it. In the first place, it degrades the name of the borrower, whoever he may be, and in the second, a loan is a loan. I ask You my Lord in the humblest way I can think of to give me strength. You can do it without any difficulty, I am sure. I will, with Your help and guidance, of course, do my best. Does Your silence mean disapproval, my Lord? I haven't sinned: I am just following my own intuition to get good answers for my actions.'

After saying her prayers, she came inside. Aowralla opened her eyes and smiled.

'Are you well?' Ebla asked. Aowralla nodded.

'Do you need anything? Water or milk? For you or for the child?' Aowralla shook her head. Ebla thought: 'I don't know why, but I wish I were in her place, giving birth (or is it life?) to a beautiful baby like that. But one should be happy with what one has. Good things and bad go side by side, fashioning one in unexpected ways, sometimes demolishing, sometimes blemishing. Just in the way that life was in my hands, crying, weeping, moving out from within Aowralla's womb, struggling its way on to the open. But one day the death of this organism is bound to come: good things and bad are bound to follow each other, just as the day is bound to follow the night. But. I'll shape the bad to be like the good – with God's help and guidance. Amen!'

7

She woke up next morning,

dreading the day that lay ahead of her. She rubbed her eyes, but was too lazy to get up and wash her face or take a bath, even though she had not washed herself since she arrived in the town. She glanced at the dirty robe she was wearing. From outside she heard the sound of water splashing.

The murmurs she heard confirmed what she had guessed: her cousin was performing his ablutions before he said his morning prayers. She turned over on her stomach to face the open door. Then she could see him lifting his arms to his ears and mumbling something like the Koran. He knelt down, then up he went and down again, until he sat down with his legs underneath the rest of his body, bringing out his forefinger as if pointing at her. She recalled that one should not lie in front of a person who is saying his prayers, otherwise he will die. There was also the fear that she might distract his attention while he was praying, but after a few minutes he came in.

He was bare-footed, and entered quietly, softly, lest they should be disturbed. He saw Ebla flickering her eyes at him and round about her.

'How was last night?' he asked her.

'Fine,' she said.

'And the kid?'

'I think, fine. It cried and cried almost all night. And Aowralla felt uncomfortable two or three times. She bled.'

'Has the bleeding stopped now?'

'I think it has.'

All this time, she had been lying in bed. She had not enough energy to stir out of bed.

'I have just come to see how they are. I will go back to the shop as soon as I have had my breakfast. Maybe I will come for lunch.'

'Breakfast' was a town-word and also a town-meal. In the country, people only ate two meals, the first of the day at noon-time. The cowherds naturally ate earlier than those who stayed back in the dwellings. This meal consisted of nothing but milk. Just occasionally they would cook thick porridge, and once in a blue moon they would eat the meat of a beast roasted for some sort of festivity, either one of the Ids, the birthday of Prophet Mohamed or a wedding ceremony. So what did this '*Qura*' and '*Qado*' mean? she asked herself.

'Just make some tea,' he said.

'What?' she asked him.

'Make some tea for the two of us.'

'And what about her?'

'Make her some porridge when she wakes up. Milk the cows and add some milk and sugar also.'

Ebla made the tea and served it to him, without milk. Then she went and milked one of the cows, brought her cousin some milk and disappeared again into the cot of the cows.

As soon as he had finished drinking, he went out. As he was leaving, he called to her, 'The lady in the next house will show you where the shop is.' Ebla was busy milking and did not say anything.

Her cousin had gone and Ebla had finished milking the cows. It was now about seven. The lady from next door came to take the cows to the place in town where the common cowherds (who charged a shilling a cow per month) would meet them. The lady, whom Ebla hadn't looked at closely, said she would return to see how Aowralla and the child were as soon as she had taken the cows to that place, after which, she added, she would take Ebla to her cousin's shop.

Ebla started preparing the porridge and poured some unboiled milk into it and stirred it up. When she had finished the preparation she went inside to see if Aowralla was awake and found that she was.

'How are you?' she asked her.

'Fine,' moaned Aowralla.

The baby was lying beside her. Her breasts were swollen, full with milk; maybe they would burst, thought Ebla. They had already begun leaking and the milk was dripping out on to the cloth which covered Aowralla. She had her legs wide apart and a little below her knees the cloth was dark with blood, the blood which she had discharged during the night. Her lips were swollen and dry and she had cracks on them. Her head-scarf was unknotted, lying behind her head; part of it had become entwined in her hair, probably because of the way she was continually turning over in he bed.

Ebla stood erect, though she was tired. She wanted to help, if only she could. But could she, she asked herself?

'Water,' said Aowralla. Ebla brought her some. Aowralla stretched her arm to take the glass and drink it herself. Her hand trembled and fell short. Ebla lifted the glass to Aowralla's lips, at the same time raising Aowralla's head from below with her hand. (Aowralla would not have been able to sit up, had she tried.)

Aowralla took a few sips, then, when the water had cooled her throat, she thanked God.

In the meantime, the baby woke up and cried. Aowralla felt an agonizing sensation. Ebla had gone away to bring her some porridge which she knew she would have to force down Aowralla's throat, since she had no appetite. However, she rushed back in when she heard the baby crying. 'Oh, my Allah,' she thought, as she stood helplessly there staring at Aowralla trying to quieten the baby, who had been uncovered by her mother.

'She is beautiful,' thought Ebla. But what did she know about babies?

'Water,' appealed Aowralla.

'Maybe that is all she can say,' Ebla thought, 'Is it possible that she has forgotten the language?'

She brought some water and handed the glass to Aowralla. After a little bit of jerking hands, re-positioning herself, turning on to one side, Aowralla managed to pour some water into the mouth of the child, who moved her lips. 'After all, she is alive and also beautiful,' thought Ebla. 'What a beautiful niece.'

Again Aowralla motioned to her. She told her to lift the baby and then whispered to her to remove the sheets from underneath the bed. They were wet with urine. As she removed them, Ebla remembered hearing that a girl's urine stank more awfully than that of boys. She laid the sheets outside in the sun to dry.

'I will bring you some porridge,' Ebla said. 'I have prepared it for you.' Aowralla nodded.

'But there is no sugar,' added Ebla. Aowralla again nodded. 'Is there?' asked Ebla. She nodded a third time. 'Where?'

Aowralla pointed to somewhere underneath the table. Ebla had dished out the porridge and had mixed in the sugar when she heard someone coming.

'Is anyone in?' asked a woman's voice.

'Come in,' replied Ebla. Ebla looked up. The woman's feet stopped a few inches from where Ebla was squatting, as she poured the porridge from one vessel to another to make it cool.

'*Nabad*,' said the woman.

'*Nabad*,' said Ebla. It was the woman who had taken the cows down to the cowherds. She was tall and extremely attractive. She was wearing what Ebla thought to be town dress, a frock, with a skirt below that and a shawl. Ebla later learnt that she was a widow, and they were to become intimate friends, but she dreaded this encounter.

'How is she?' the woman whispered, as if the question was something secretive.

'Fine,' replied Ebla, as usual.

'Asleep?' asked the woman. Ebla nodded. She thought she would get rid of her. She did not like seeing her there and she feared that the sight of her might make Aowralla's wounds worse. The woman disappeared, but before going she said that she would come back again to take Ebla to the shop.

Ebla gave Aowralla her porridge. Then, after a while, Aowralla fell asleep. The baby had fallen asleep an hour or so before. Later on, the woman came to take Ebla to the shop.

8

Ebla and the widow walked along

as if they were tied together. It annoyed Ebla no end to wade
through a crowd like that. Yesterday she had not been aware
of it, but today it was an effort being in that dress, which the
widow had helped her into, as her robe was very dirty. It
had more loose ends and she felt naked: it was entirely different from her own robe – not like a robe at all. It was six
metres long, instead of twelve, and it was kept on by knotting
the loose edge with a folded piece, putting this round the
neck, and wrapping the remaining parts around her.

Her cousin's shop was not very far away. The widow had
made her expect quite a long walk, but to her half a mile was
nothing.

When they were inside the shop she looked round to see
what was for sale. She saw what looked to her like a wumpum,
hanging somewhere near the ceiling. Underneath, there were
piles and piles of old Italian journals used as sugar-holders,
tea-holders and such like. Heaps of unused (but dusty and
old) exercise books lay elsewhere. These meant nothing to
Ebla. On the table, which took up quite a lot of space in the
shop, and served as a partition between her cousin, the shop-
keeper, and the customers, there were various vessels, which
differed in size, colour and ugliness. One contained sesame
oil, one kerosene oil and one coffee seeds. To the right of her
cousin some sugar-containers lay side by side.

'Two kilos of sugar,' said a woman customer.

'Twenty cents of sugar,' said a young girl. The orders

went on and on. Everybody spoke as if he was the only one talking and as if he thought he ought not to have to wait for the others in the shop to place their orders. Ebla's cousin dashed here and there, trying to please his customers as best he could. He had not seen Ebla and the widow come in.

Then a young girl came in to return the oil which she had bought, or rather said she had bought from him. How could he remember who had bought what in such a fantastically busy shop?

'Go back to your mother and tell her that the shopkeeper said that he wouldn't take it back,' as he busied himself.

'But I bought it from you,' the young girl cried.

It was only when the widow tried to comfort the young girl, that Ebla's cousin noticed that they had come. He did not say another word. His eyes met Ebla's and he stopped as if trying to recall where he had placed a certain thing. He dashed back, put his hands in a glass full of coins, counted some and gave them to Ebla.

'Go to the next shop and get the spaghetti,' he said.

'Get what from the next shop?' asked Ebla, receiving the money from him with both hands.

'She knows what it is,' said he, pointing at the widow. 'The man in the next shop has an account for me. After you have taken the packet of spaghetti, you will go to the butcher's and buy some meat,' he continued. 'You help her, will you?' he said, addressing the widow. All this in a hurry.

'Yes, I will,' the widow said.

The widow took Ebla by the arm and led her away. They went into the next shop, and collected the packet of spaghetti, then Ebla followed the widow to the butcher's shop and they bought half a kilo of meat.

Ebla followed the widow back to the house. At the door, the widow said she had better go to her house. She promised she would return very soon and help Ebla to cook the lunch.

Ebla could hear the baby crying the moment she stepped into the house. She walked lamely and now she cursed herself for coming to the town.

Aowralla was standing on her feet, wobbling on a stick, knitting her brows because of the pain. She was trying to get milk for the baby, but she could not move. She could neither keep on standing nor sit down: she was in a helpless position. The blood had dried in between her thighs and the hair which grew there had increased the stiffness of the limbs. With the basket still in her hands, Ebla rushed forward to assist Aowralla.

'What do you want?' she asked Aowralla, gripping her by the shoulders.

'I have been attempting to get the milk for the baby.' The baby had still not stopped crying.

'Sit down,' said Ebla.

'I cannot,' was Aowralla's reply.

'Can you keep on standing for a while?' Aowralla nodded. 'Do that, then,' said Ebla, putting down the basket on the floor. 'Now, look. Lean against me. Like that. Yes. Good.' Ebla gripped her by the arm-pit, which was wet, and moved away one step. Aowralla leaned against her, feeling the numbing pain in her thighs. 'Thrust yourself forward gently now ... slowly.' Aowralla did so. Ebla pulled her a little more. The strain on Aowralla's stiff thighs had eased now and she was able gradually to lean against Ebla's shoulder, until she could lie flat on her back.

'But you did not eat the porridge,' said Ebla, going to get some milk for the baby. She really did not care any longer – these things were getting on her nerves.

Aowralla stammered something. Ebla helped the baby to drink, placing it on her lap, then lifting its head and pouring the milk into its mouth. The baby was silent and closed her eyes.

'Maybe she needs to sleep,' said her mother.

'She should,' said Ebla dismissing the topic.

'Were you able to buy the things?'

'Yes.'

'How was he? Very busy?'

'Yes, he was.'

'The widow was quite helpful?'

'Yes, she was.'

'Do you know how to cook spaghetti?'

'You mean the thing in the paper?'

'Yes.'

'I have never seen it before.'

'Tear it open now,' said Aowralla.

'Now or later?'

'Now.'

Ebla tore the packet open and some long white hollow rods came out. Unintentionally, she broke a few of them. She thought that they should not be broken and put the broken pieces aside.

Aowralla smiled at what she saw, but Ebla could not understand. 'Give it to me,' said Aowralla.

'The packet?'

'Yes'.

Ebla stood up and handed the packet over to Aowralla.

Aowralla broke the things into pieces and gave them back to Ebla who hesitatingly accepted them.

'Boil some water. And you put everything in when the water has boiled. That is how we eat spaghetti: it is very simple, and my husband likes it that way,' said Aowralla. 'But don't cook it now: only when he is about to come for lunch. You can cut the meat now and cook it. Cut it into small pieces, then wash them. Then cut the onions, grind the garlics and cut the tomatoes also.'

'I don't know what you are talking about,' said Ebla.

'Get a big plate and come near me. I will show you. Empty the whole packet into the plate.' Ebla did as she was told.

Aowralla said that the garlics were missing and asked Ebla to go and get some. But the widow came, and said she had forgotten to buy them, but that she had some in her house, so she went and got a handful.

When cooked, the meat was delicious, but Ebla could not bear looking at the spaghetti. She merely picked at it. 'Tapeworms. How can I eat tapeworms?' she asked herself.

Her cousin came back and devoured the meal. He did not stay long, but went back immediately to the shop. 'It is the marketing session,' he said.

After Aowralla and the baby had both fallen asleep, Ebla returned to the widow's house next door.

9

Ebla still had a bitter taste in
her mouth. She wished she could stick to her previous
milk-meat meals and occasionally some thick porridge. But
she was in town, not in the country, where she had been all
her life, where she had never helped at child-birth and where
she had never acted as an errand-girl. What a miserable life!

She pushed the main door open and walked in. It was the
first time she had visited the widow, although the widow
had hinted that she could go any time to her place, to ask for
help in her cousin's house-keeping or for anything else. She
walked gracefully with her robe round her body, striding
along like a queen. She looked back when she heard a bang,
but it was only the outer door closing: the noise had
frightened her. At the widow's door, Ebla waited motionless for she could hear a man's voice from inside.

'How are Aowralla and her husband?' asked the man's
voice.

'Fine. Aowralla has given birth to a child.'

'Oh, she has, has she?'

'Yes.'

'A girl or a boy?'

'A girl.'

'I guess he needs it.'

'And there is a newcomer. A cousin of his just turned up
yesterday and was in time to help.'

'And will she go back?'

'I don't know for certain.'

'What does she look like?'

'Well, I cannot say.'

'She is not worth calling a woman?'

'No. I think she is very beautiful, except she looks like a spinster.'

'How old do you think she is?'

'I cannot say.'

'I like spinsters anyway. They will bless the day you were born, and children and milk and meat and prosperity will come in plenty. They come in handy when one needs a woman to marry. They don't say no, because it would mean more years to languish through and more agony to pass through. And more "scratching" for them also. I like my wife to be older than myself.'

'I imagine this one is not.'

'What is her name?'

'Ebla.'

'Good name,' he said and clucked like a donkey-guide.

Ebla stood at the door with her hand resting on the handle. The main gate had opened and closed before she could see who came in. And when she did, she saw somebody in a dark veil looking towards her. She almost ran away, but she decided to wait. Was it a man? Or was it a woman? Or a ghost? Or a genie? 'Oh, my Lord, come and help.' When the person in the veil was a few paces away from where Ebla stood, afraid, but adventurous and bold, he stopped. The eyes of the person peeping through the two holes deliberately made to serve as inlets made Ebla more frightened. Ebla examined 'the object', 'the thing', 'the person' up and down. The person stopped where he was. Then Ebla looked at the shoes: they were unlike any shoes she had ever seen. 'It must be a ghost that has come to capture me,' she thought. 'My grandfather has cursed me. My brother doesn't want to see me any more. I have left

Aowralla and the baby alone,' she told herself. 'But I must do something.'

She lifted her robe with the tips of her fingers, then looked all around her. She looked at the person again. The eyes were still staring at her through the two holes. She closed her eyes and imagined herself to be elsewhere, to be a kid again, playing 'Catch the thief' and she ran. The person in the veil gave way and she passed by him swiftly, hitting him with her long arm. She opened the main door of the widow's house in a hurry and rushed into her cousin's house to talk to Aowralla about it.

Aowralla and the baby were both asleep. Ebla wondered why she had not raised her little finger and said 'A *udu billahi mina el shaidani rajim*,' which would supposedly protect her from the ghost or genie. She wished she had stayed in the country and never left; only, country life was more monotonous than that in the town.

She looked at herself, at her robe, at the motif on her dress, at the beautiful colours that were painted on the robe. She had always wanted to wear a robe like this. Once she had almost got one: a woman had brought it with her, and decided to sell it to her, second hand, but then had decided against it. Again she felt the robe with her fingers.

But the ghost. 'What did it want from me?' Who could be the man inside? Surely he was not courting her? But how could she know? All she knew about the woman next door was that she had been a widow for three years and was now over thirty. This meant that she was beyond the age of marriage, Ebla thought. And if this man was ever keen on the widow, would he talk to her about another woman? And if he wanted to marry a woman older than he why didn't he marry the widow? She must be older than he, Ebla thought. Could he be a relation? Could he be the brother of the widow? Everything was possible.

Ebla then saw that Aowralla had woken from her sleep. Aowralla licked her lips. They were dry, stiff and swollen.

'Water,' she mumbled. Ebla brought the water and then Aowralla went back to sleep.

Ebla lay down on the spring bed which had frightened her the previous day, but only to relax. However, she fell asleep. When she woke up the baby was crying and Aowralla was moving, but soon they were asleep again. Ebla had her eyes half open. Her ears quivered. As the superstition goes, she thought that someone was talking about her somewhere far away. She did not have to think who those people could be – she hardly knew anybody except her relatives in the country; one never went out of one's way to make acquaintances in the country. But what could they be saying about her? Or was her grandfather sick? She could not continue thinking about her grandfather, for she knew that his situation must have worsened by now, and could be very serious. 'He might even have died, for all I know,' she said. And it would be much better for him and the others around him and anyone who loved him if he had. 'What is life if one outlives it? It is much more comforting to die when one is talking than when one starts to mumble.'

Although she tried to reason with herself as to whether or not she should have left, she could not come to any conclusion. 'I left the country and am in town, so why worry about it any more,' she told herself. At least, she told this to the part of her personality which required an explanation or apology for her stay in town. Something within herself had been wanting to have similar queries answered, but the reply was not of any consequence. She must make whatever she could from where she was.

She had never been a split personality, but she had seemed slightly uncertain. The first time that she saw a car she was almost petrified on the spot. And it was only this afternoon that she had been asked to take the radio to her cousin. Her cousin had put it on and Dalais was singing. Ebla went round the radio and touched it on all corners; she thought someone must be inside – a woman, since she could recognize the voice was that of a woman. But all the same, she did not want to expose her ignorance to the others. She left those things with the hope that she would learn about them at a later date. She would do whatever the townspeople did. And by this process, she would learn.

After some time, her palms itched. 'Someone will give me some money,' she thought. She was still toying with this idea when the baby cried and the mother awoke also.

'Milk,' again.

'Water,' again.

10

There was a knock on the outside

door. Ebla heard the knock, but waited to be sure. The
tapping continued, a soft rap. Aowralla sat up and lifted the
glass to her mouth. The baby cried; Aowralla, instead of
drinking the water herself, gave it to the baby.

Meanwhile, Ebla went to answer the door. She hesitated,
uncertain whether or not she should open the door. However, she heard the widow's familiar voice from behind the
closed door.

'Open it. It's me.' Ebla opened the door.

'Did you come to my house?' asked the widow, standing
in the doorway.

'Yes.'

'Is Aowralla awake?' she asked, changing the subject,
which infuriated Ebla.

'Yes.'

'Is she fine?'

'Yes.'

'I want to go and talk to her then.'

Ebla followed the widow inside. One could never tell
which was the guest – the widow striding powerfully along
or Ebla following her. They looked like Cleopatra and one
of the million slaves she kept.

Even before they were inside, the widow said, 'Aowralla, it
is your turn to collect the Shollingo, but you haven't paid for
a couple of days. That means two shillings less. Is that right?'

'I think it is.'

The widow walked away without looking back again. Even when she said good-bye, she walked straight ahead, occasionally looking down at the ground as if she were walking on thorn-bushes. She lifted her leg, as if she meant to kick them off: she threw them forward. Her face was magnificent. A widow, this one? One would be tempted to say, 'Married twice. Divorced once. Left in the lurch once' – or perhaps he had died before she walked out.

'Come, Ebla. Close the door,' she said authoritatively, Ebla obediently followed her. The widow made some jingling sound with the coins she kept in her hands. She threw them up one or two at a time. 'Why did you run away?' asked the widow, facing Ebla.

'What?'

'Why did you run away? I just asked you.'

'When?'

'When you came to my house.'

'This afternoon?'

'Yes.'

'I did not run away.'

'You did. You did run away.'

'How do you know?'

'Because I know.'

'How?'

'I don't have to say.'

'Did you see from a hole or something? The hole in the wall?' Ebla asked, meaning the window.

The widow said, 'No.'

The widow took the door handle and swung it to and fro, making a creaking sound that was unpleasant to hear. The wind blew up the widow's frock and she stopped to cover herself immediately. She looked up and her eyes met Ebla's. Ebla was silent, just staring at the widow, who now gave a shy smile.

'My friend saw you,' said the widow.

'Who saw me?'

'My Arab friend.'

'So you have Arabs down here?' asked Ebla, quite interested in pursuing the issue.

'Yes. Many of them.'

'And the one who saw me? But how come, I did not see him.' Ebla was afraid. That reminded her of the ghost that she had seen. 'But that might be the friend that she is talking about,' she thought to herself.

'She was in a dark veil.'

'Oh, was that an Arab?' Ebla asked, moving away from the widow.

Ebla sneezed then moved a bit forward and blew her nose with her fingers, flicked off the mucus into the air (it narrowly missed the widow) and then wiped her fingers on her robe.

'Yes,' answered the widow.

'A man or a woman?'

'A woman.'

'Oh, I would like to meet an Arab.'

'Why?'

'Because they are the Prophet's relatives. They are nearer to him than we are, aren't they?'

'They are not the Prophet's relatives any more than we are. I don't know what they are.'

'Do they speak Arabic?'

'Yes. I guess they do speak something like it.'

'Then they speak the language of the Koran?'

'No, they don't.'

'What do they speak?'

'The rumour is that these we have in Somalia were the blacksmiths in Arabia.'

'Who told you?'

'My first husband was an Arab.'

'Oh, was he?'

'Yes, and he made me cover myself with veils, as dark as coal. Well, that is what our religion requires – that women should cover the whole body. I don't see anything wrong in that. He was a nice man,' she added.

The widow had now gone beyond the stage of keeping secrets. The talk interested Ebla more than she had ever realized it could.

'My husband was as jealous as a monkey,' said the widow of a sudden, in a matter-of-fact way.

'Like what?' asked Ebla.

'A monkey.'

'In what way?'

'Did you hear about the story of the monkeys?'

'I have heard many stories about monkeys.'

'Did you hear what they do to their females?'

'Well, I suppose they don't eat them, do they?'

'No. Far from it.'

Ebla was silent and the widow added, 'Guess what they do to them?'

'They make love to them?' asked Ebla in a low voice, and looked around her. 'Oh, my God, what did I say?' thought Ebla inwardly.

'Yes. But what besides that?' said the widow in a cool voice.

'I don't know.'

'Well they cover the "thing" with sticky, wet mud before they leave her. The whole area and its neighbouring area, I mean.'

'What does that symbolize?'

'That will enable them to know whether or not the female has been made love to during the male monkey's absence.'

'How does the poor animal know?'

'You mean the monkey?'

'Yes.'

'You should know.'

'But I don't know.'

'He sniffs at it, you idiot.'

'Is that all?'

'No. He also looks at it. If the "thing" is wet, and there is an opening then he beats her like the devil.'

'Now how did your Arab husband resemble a monkey?'

'They are both jealous.'

'Was yours very jealous?'

'Yes, that is why he divorced me. He thought I was sleeping with other men. He could not speak Somali, although he stayed in this country throughout his life. And whenever I spoke to anyone in Somali, he would think that I dated him. If it was a woman, he would think that she was a procurer.'

'Do you speak Arabic then?'

'Yes, very little. Enough to get me another Arab, if I were interested in them. Well, I suppose I'd better go. My nephew is waiting for me in the house. He is all by himself.'

'Is this man in the house your nephew?'

'Yes. And he is such a lovely man.'

'*Nabadgalio* – good-bye,' said the widow, rushing through the door.

'*Nabadino* – good-bye to you too,' replied Ebla.

II

Ebla's cousin had been involved
in a smuggling racket. Kallafo was about a hundred miles
away. He kept an agent to smuggle goods into the territory
from Kallafo, and he sold these to the people in the area.
Today was the day the goods would arrive.

Ebla had just closed the door, when she heard an exchange
of greetings between her cousin and the widow. She came
back and opened the door.

'How is she?' he said, walking past her.

'Fine.'

'And the kid?' he said.

'Also fine,' she said.

He looked backward as he entered the room. Ebla followed
him. Quite understandingly, his wife said:

'Is everything all right?'

'Yes.'

'When is it?'

'In about two to three hours.'

'Who are you going with?'

'With some of my friends,' he replied.

Aowralla was silent.

'How is the kid?'

'Fine,' she said.

'Does she disturb you?'

'No. Not very much.'

Ebla stood in the doorway. She looked at her cousin,

puzzled. He kept opening one drawer after another. He could not find whatever he was searching for.

'Where is it?'

Aowralla must have known what he was looking for, for she answered:

'In the crate.'

'Why didn't you tell me?'

'Did you ask me?'

'But you knew what I was searching for.'

'Anyway, get it from the crate.'

'Where is the crate? I mean which crate?'

'The black one,' Aowralla replied.

'Which black one?'

'We have only got one black crate. The other one is brown, and it is no good. It doesn't even close.'

Ebla's cousin moved towards the boxes which lay upon each other like dead animals. He lifted the two boxes and then came to the crates, which he opened. He looked round to see if anyone was watching. Ebla shamefacedly cast down her eyes when they met his bloodshot ones.

'That must be a pistol,' she thought – and it was.

Her cousin re-arranged the boxes as they were, on top of each other, with the black crate underneath. He took out his handkerchief and wiped away the dust from his shirt and cleaned his hands also.

Ebla knew that she would not hesitate to help her cousin. But how could she? She did not know what his intentions were. She knew, however, that there must have been a good reason why he needed a pistol. She was a woman, and she ought not to interfere with the jobs of males. 'But his wife knows about it. As soon as he spoke about it, she directed him where to find it.'

'Ebla, the cows have come back. I hear their mooing. Go to them. And don't let the calves suck them.'

Ebla ran to attend to them. She fed the cows with grass. Then she heard her cousin calling to her again, urgently. He asked her to go and call the widow, which she did.

'I am taking Ebla with me. Will you milk the cows for the baby and her mother?' her cousin enquired of the widow.

'I have a guest. I must prepare dinner for him, but I think I can milk one cow for the baby and the mother. When Ebla comes back maybe she can milk the rest,' replied the widow.

'Good. Milk one for them.'

'Yes. I will,' replied the widow, looking at Ebla who stood statue-like, wondering what was happening.

'My nephew, Awill, came this afternoon,' said the widow, fixing her eyes on Ebla.

'Did he?' asked Ebla's cousin.

'Yes.'

'Give him my salaams. I will see him when I come home, I think.'

The widow took leave immediately after that, and shouted to Aowralla from outside to say that she would come and milk the cow. Aowralla had no intention of answering back.

'Let us hurry, Ebla. There is not much time,' said her cousin. He went inside to say goodbye to his wife.

'Allah be on your shoulders. Go under his protection, amen,' said his wife.

'Go with him, Ebla. And be careful,' Aowralla added to her husband.

'Yes.'

Ebla was to a certain extent doubtful about what was going to happen, but she did not want to show this to her cousin or to anyone else for that matter. She was willing to get entangled in any situation as long as it would help her cousin and his wife. She walked behind him, losing courage now, then regaining it; hesitating whether or not she should run these risks, but then convincing herself in the same

61

breath that whatever this was that she had become involved in would benefit her cousin.

Ebla and her cousin walked side by side. They stopped abruptly just after they had passed the Arch at Belet Amin. Her cousin looked around suspiciously. He told her to wait for him on the pavement (the road was the main and only one in town and it was asphalt). She said that she would.

Two men in what were to Ebla strange outfits stopped nearby. After a little while, her cousin came out of the building he had entered with three men who Ebla thought unusual in appearance, clad in khaki uniforms. They walked hurriedly away. Ebla's cousin came up to her and whispered, 'Come, follow us.' She had never in all her life been as frightened as she was this evening. She had handled wounded persons, she had assisted in cutting off the hand of a fellow-peasant, when a bullet lodged there, she had attended to young girls undergoing the circumcision operation, she had cut off the useless ear of a calf when there were no males to do the job, but she had never been face to face with wars and never had a duel fight. As a woman, that was quite outside her experience. This lack of knowledge about what was to happen increased the tension in her.

Before she divulged her utter confusion (for she had never been to that side of town), she saw the other three men entering a house. Her cousin stopped.

'You wait here. I will come back in a minute,' he said to her, then headed towards the entrance. She did this, then immediately afterwards he came out, his arms swaying with an extremely heavy load. A cloth was wrapped around some items. Ebla noticed that her cousin could not walk properly. He staggered with the heavy load on his shoulders. He moved one leg at a time to balance the other.

'Take this to the house,' he commanded.

'Our house?' Ebla asked.

'Yes, ours,' he said with obvious contempt.

'But I don't know . . .' she started innocently.

'Lift the thing first, you fool. I will give you directions to the house,' he said.

He transferred the load to her back. And then munched the words as he gave her the directions to his house. She was supposed to go straight until she came to a big old fig tree on the side of the road. After that she should take the first road to the right, and the house would be the fourth from the corner.

Ebla touched the load. There was something mysterious about it, but it was not as heavy as she had expected; she had carried heavier things than that. It was only when she reached their gate that she changed the position of the load so that she could enter.

The widow had just finished milking the cow and was in a hurry, she said. Ebla found Aowralla and the baby awake.

She unloaded herself.

'How was it?' asked Aowralla.

'What?' said Ebla.

'The thing. Where was he? I mean when you left him.'

'He was entering a house. He had walked towards the entrance when I turned my back to him.'

'Was he alone?'

'No.'

'How many?'

'Three others.'

'Did the others come with you?'

'No. They were inside.'

'May God help them,' said Aowralla.

'Amen,' joined in Ebla.

But she wished she knew what the load that she had carried contained. She had tried several times to guess what it was. It could have been maize or gold, for all she knew.

Why would maize be hidden and brought into the house only when it got dark?

Ebla had performed her routine tasks of milking the cows – one less, thanks to the widow – and rubbing the milk-container with pieces of coal. ('But why do people brush their teeth with coal? And why do pregnant women chew clay?' Ebla asked herself.) The main door was thrown open and her cousin came in panting, beads of sweat had accumulated on his forehead.

'What happened?' asked his wife.

'They caught it.'

'All of it.'

'Yes, all of it.'

'And the other men?'

'Yes, the other men also.'

'What about you?'

'I ran for my life. They almost fired at me.'

'You would not fire back, I knew.'

'It was the two men who had been watching you who followed us. If only I had not taken you with me,' he said to Ebla. Ebla did not utter a word.

'It is Ebla who saved you this much, otherwise you would have nothing left with you. Thank Allah. You fool,' said Aowralla.

'I will hit you if you say another word.'

'And you,' he said to Ebla, 'Get out of my sight. I hope I will never see you again.'

Ebla walked out of the house in a foul mood. Inside, she blamed herself, but she justified his genuine fury. Since she knew nobody else, she went to the widow's house.

12

Ebla could hardly knock on the
widow's door. Somehow or other, she thought that the
widow would refuse her the milk of human kindness, which
she was always seeking. She never expected anyone to be
grateful to her, neither would she want anyone to be annoyed
with her. Innumerable ghost-like sights seemed to hover
around her. A spasm of hatred seeped into her. But whom
did she hate? And did she ever love anyone in her life? The
ghost that she had seen the previous day had turned out to
be a person – an Arab woman, which made the incident
screamingly funny. She wondered then if she had ever been
on the right track. She had been reticent all her life, because
it turned out that her opinions were different from what
others expected. 'That proves either that I am an exceptional
idiot, or the reverse.'

One question after another leapt into her mind. Questions
made her situation worse. They touched the sores and turned
them (figuratively speaking) into big wounds; the wounds
which had been (or appeared to be) healing for the four days
she had stayed in town.

On second thoughts, Ebla decided to return. 'No, I should
not see her. Why should I?' she thought. Something inside
her suggested that she should go back to her cousin's house
and see if he had left; then she would sleep and would see
what the morning brought. Turning around, she saw the
widow coming.

'Is that you?' asked the widow.

'Yes, it is me,' replied Ebla.

'Did you hear?'

Ebla nodded.

'It is horrible.'

'What?' she enquired distantly.

Ebla had no idea what the whole incident was about. Her cousin had rebuked her, but as far as she was concerned, she was innocent. She did not want to hear any more about it, for the thought that she had upset her cousin, and his wife coaxed her into unnecessary dejection.

'The bastards,' the widow exclaimed.

'Who?'

'The Police.'

'But who are they?'

'How can I explain to somebody like you? In a town like Belet Wene, we have Police.'

'Is it the name of a tribe?'

'Maybe in a way.'

'I have never heard the name of this tribe. Under which main sect do they come?'

'Did you hear about Government?'

'No. Another tribe?'

'No. No. No. In towns, we don't talk in terms of tribes. We talk in terms of societies. You see, in this town, there are many different tribes who live together. Have you ever seen a white man?'

'No. I have never seen a white man, God's curse be on him. Why should I?'

'Well, you see, the Government is the white man. Did you hear anybody talking about Independence?'

'No. I heard about the Abyssinians, the Arabs and the Kikuyus, but I have never seen any of them. I saw one *Amhar* when we were dwelling somewhere near Kallafo.'

'Look, Ebla, we cannot talk about these things outside here. Let us go in and talk it over. My nephew has not come back.' When they were inside, the widow explained to Ebla in detail all about the Police, Government, the white man, and the Independence of Somalia, which was approaching. After explaining all this and hearing what had befallen Ebla, the widow told her to rest there for a while.

After some time, the widow's nephew came. Ebla and the widow were sitting in the room, which was dimly lit. The hurricane lamp had probably run out of kerosene. The shops were closed by then and the widow did not intend to see if the neighbours had any kerosene to lend.

Ebla looked up to see what had darkened the room. 'Maybe there is someone standing in the doorway,' she thought. Then she saw a tall man, slim and handsome, looking into her face. The little light which fell upon his face hardly showed his features. However, Awill (for that was his name) greeted them.

'*Nabad.*'

'*Nabad,*' said the widow, smiling at her nephew.

'And who could this be?' he said in a sombre voice that bewildered Ebla. It was strange and remote.

'This is Ebla,' said the widow.

'She is from next door, is she?'

'Yes,' replied the widow.

'How long have you been in town, Ebla?'

Ebla did not say anything.

The widow answered for her.

'Is she mute?' said Awill addressing his aunt. As if he changed his mind, he addressed her this time, 'Are you?'

'No,' she said. 'I talk. But don't talk unless it is necessary.'

'Quite interesting,' he said.

The widow then said that she must go out, but that she

would come back soon. Awill moved over so that she could pass.

He walked forward into the room and reached out for a chair, but not the one the widow had been sitting on. He sat down in an older, shabbier chair; then he cleared his throat, which Ebla felt was meaningful, but sat as if he was not ready to say anything.

'Maybe he is waiting for me to speak,' thought Ebla. But what should I say? What? He was unlike any man whom she had talked to: it was as though, being a town-dweller, he came from another planet, and she dared not talk to him.

Courting in the country was basically the same as in town, she thought. If I had a mother and I was in our dwelling, she would have left us alone as soon as the suitor entered. The widow did just the same.

Then his voice broke in on her thoughts.

'Are you going back?'

'Where to?'

Ebla, in a fraction of a second, thought he knew what had happened between her and her cousin.

'To the country,' replied Awill.

Inwardly she was pleased with the answer.

'I don't know,' she said.

Ebla felt something crawling over her belly, creeping up towards her slender breasts. It gave her an irritating sensation. She wanted to kill the insect or whatever it was, but without attracting the attention of Awill. It seemed to her that he had a strange way of staring at her. His black eyes were fixed on her all the time, as if they were boring through her.

There was silence again, but Ebla could still feel the insect. She swallowed, simultaneously lifting her left hand to her throat to accompany down the saliva. And while his eyes were busy following the movements of her left hand, she put her right hand through the opening to the belly and searched for the insect. 'It might be a louse,' she thought. 'And what a disgrace.' By then the insect (for she never saw what it was) had landed on the valley between her breasts. Ebla killed it on the spot. It left some moisture and the corpse of the insect fell down to her belly. Ebla looked in the direction of Awill and found him looking at the ground.

After this long silence, she asked him:

'How long do you intend to stay here?'

'Nine days or so.'

'Your aunt told me that you come from *Hamar*,' said Ebla.

'Yes.'

'How big is it?'

'Fairly big.'

'Is it bigger than this town?'

'Yes. Much bigger.'

'I hope I will go there one day.'

'Let us hope you will.'

'I don't know anybody in Hamar.'

'Now you know me.'

'But you are a stranger,' she told herself.

And aloud she said:

'Yes, I know you.'

'Good.'

'What do you do in Hamar?' asked Ebla.

'I work for the Government.'

'You catch smuggled goods, is that what you do? Like some of them who caught my cousin's goods this evening?'

'No.'

'Then what do you do?' Ebla asked with a prudence foreign to her.

'I work in Publica Istruzione. But you won't understand anyway.'

'But tell me, what is your main duty?'

'That is where teachers are sent from.'

'But you are not a teacher?'

'No, I work in an office.'

She did not understand what 'an office' meant, but she thought she might leave it at that for the time being. She would learn all these things later.

'I know now,' she said.

'How do you like Belet Wene?'

'I don't know. I have not been here for long. I will be able to say when I have been here for a month.'

The widow came back. She told Ebla that she had been to her cousin's house and that Aowralla was waiting for her.

'Is he there?' Ebla asked, meaning her cousin.

'No he has gone back to the shop to sleep there.'

Ebla went back to her cousin's house. Aowralla said that she was sorry her husband had maltreated her.

'But you should not take these things seriously. It is one of his moods.'

'I won't,' Ebla assured her.

And after a little while, she was snoring her head off.

13

Ebla woke up the following
morning, feeling morbid and rather sickly. But she wasn't in
the least worried about it. 'Why should I? I am only an intruder into this world. And I could not abandon life. It has
not yielded fruits to me as yet but I always put my hopes on
the morrow. But the future is black. I have undergone an
absolute shattering of my spirit and the mirror of my existence.' She rubbed her eyes, then met those of Aowralla,
when she looked down at where the latter lay.

They exchanged '*Nabad.*'

After which Aowralla quite happily announced, 'It has
broken.'

'What has?' Ebla asked.

'The umbilical cord.'

Ebla sat up and said 'When?'

'Just now,' Aowralla replied, her voice sounding little
better. Although the sheets which served as a mattress had
not been washed, the place looked better now. The atmos-
phere no longer smelt of child-delivery, thanks largely to the
burning of the incense which was still being used to cover up
the smell. If she wanted, Aowralla could walk all by herself
to the outer door without Ebla's help. And she need not
wobble on the metallic walking stick, but she felt lazy and
seedy inside.

Ebla thought that Aowralla looked like an unfinished
ornament. She could not think in terms of many adornments,
because she had not seen many. A milk receptacle was

adorned with beads stitched on to the outside of it, straw mats were dyed in different colours. And these stitchings or paintings were arranged in various attractive patterns. Ebla thought that Aowralla needed some more touches to be added to her, but that could only be done by the Creator and He must have wanted her to be as she was – after all, there could be no greater artist. Aowralla's acquiline nose suited her big dark glowing eyes, but her eye-sockets were too hollow and too thin, and the dimples in her cheeks would look better on someone else. Her limbs were long and her height was in proportion to them. Ebla envied her dark lips, quite soft and bulging forward, as if they smiled teasingly. Her neck was long like a giraffe's and there was a scar (maybe burnt by a local medicine-man for some sickness or other) right on the hollow base of her throat.

Ebla got out of bed.

Aowralla covered the child, who was now asleep again.

'Sleeping?' asked Ebla.

'Yes,' answered Aowralla.

Aowralla raised her head, sat up (the pain was not as intense as before) and pulled the baby's umbilical cord from underneath the drapery. She stretched her hand which was shaking a little, towards Ebla, who reached out.

'Very long. It is very long,' said Ebla.

'Not very. It is normal,' said Aowralla.

Ebla knew what the people in the country did with the umbilical cords. Maybe she ought to wait until Aowralla told her what to do with it though, she thought.

'What is today?' asked Aowralla.

'I don't know.'

'What about the date?'

'No idea.'

'This is my third day.'

'Yes. Your third day.'

'What a pain!'

'But it is over now,' said Ebla. 'Console a miser to save his liver' she thought.

'And is bound to come back.'

'Only if God blesses you with them again.'

'I don't know if I will want any more.'

Aowralla looked up at Ebla, who looked even more than six foot from that angle.

'It has been a great drawback to our economy. I mean the family – including yourself,' she said.

'The widow told me.'

'What else did she tell you?'

'Many other things.'

'She is a gem of a woman.'

'I think she is.'

'Do you like her?'

'Yes.'

'But the townspeople gossip about her being a white-shoed woman.' This is a common way of saying that she was easy-going.

'I don't know much about it.'

'Well that is why her Arab husband left her.'

'She told me.'

'Did she tell you the whole story?'

'No. Only bits of it.'

'Well, she faced much trouble with that Arab fellow. He did not want to divorce her. Neither did he want her to remain his wife.'

'And then what happened?'

'Her nephew saved her.'

'Awill?'

'How do you know?'

'He is here.'

'Did you see him?'

'Yes. I saw him yesterday evening.'

'He is a charming chap.'

'I wouldn't know.'

'I know him fairly well,' said Aowralla, and as an afterthought she asked, 'How long did he say he is going to stay?'

'Six days. I think he said that.'

'He wanted to marry an Arab girl himself. She was a spinster, but she was the sister of the widow's husband. So the Arab wanted to get her married off to Awill. It was after the trouble that the project failed.'

'Is he married?'

'I don't know. You never know with people from *Hamar*. Only God knows whether or not they are married, but I don't think they are, otherwise I would have heard about it.'

'I guess so.'

The baby began to cry. Her mother turned over, so that her breast could dangle out to her mouth. Ebla could hear the sound of the baby's sucking.

'Do you have the umbilical cord?'

'Yes. Here it is.'

The cord was dry, but moist inside. Pressing it with her fingers, Ebla could feel the thing breathing. Now that it was going to be disposed of, she amused herself fingering it.

Then Aowralla told Ebla:

'Tie it round the ear of Bafto.'

'Yes. I will.'

Hardly five minutes had passed when Ebla's cousin entered the house. He looked at her angrily. If she could, she would have run away and never see him again.

'How is it?' asked his wife.

'Very bad.'

'Do they know whose goods they are?'

'Yes.'

'How?'

'Because they caught one of the coolies.'

'Where is he now?'

'In prison.'

'And did he give you away?'

'Yes.'

'Well, why shouldn't he?' said Aowralla.

'Why should he?'

'They are not his goods, are they?'

'Anyway, I am in trouble.'

'Why didn't you go back to the shop and work as a normal man?'

'I have got to pay them. And I have also got to pay money to the man from whom I bought the goods.'

'How are you going to manage that?'

'Maybe I will sell one or two of the cows.'

'Yes. But that doesn't seem to solve the problem.'

'It does. If only a little.'

'Which of the cows? There are only four of them. The rest have died or been eaten by hyenas.'

'Bafto is the only cow which can sell well.'

'I have just offered Bafto as a navel-knotted-present to the baby. You should not sell it.'

'Who did the tying?'

'Ebla did.'

Ebla thought to herself 'God save me.'

'She is an ominous person. If she were not with us, we would not have been caught. I have always dealt in smuggled goods and nothing has happened before. It is because of her.'

'But don't you care for the baby?'

'It doesn't know anything about it. This is a question of survival. And dignity. And prestige.'

'But the baby's feelings! Although she is only three days old, she will hear about this.'

'She won't. Unless you tell her.'

'Yes, I will tell her.'

'You can tell her. By then we will have either gone down or up in the scale of life.'

Ebla's eyes met those of her cousin. Because her face was directed towards him he said, 'Why are you looking at me like that? It is my baby, my cows and the problem is between me and my wife.'

Having said this, he walked away. On the same day, before lunch, he sold Bafto.

Later on, Ebla had just milked the remaining cows and had her back resting lazily against the door when her cousin came in. He was happy and in high spirits. This was the opposite of what Ebla and Aowralla had expected. He told them that the goods had been confiscated by the police and that they had fined him a thousand shillings or so, and warned him that next time he was caught, he would be put in prison for two years with hard labour and the fine would depend on the value of the smuggled goods. Each of the women had been weeping inside, though occasionally Ebla would sob and Aowralla would comfort her.

'It is not true, is it?' Aowralla said.

'What?' her husband asked.

'That you have been fined.'

'Not as much as a thousand.'

Ebla always kept quiet when Aowralla and her husband discussed their family affairs, and unless spoken to, she never uttered a single word. She knew that she was not expected to say anything.

'You've sold the cow?'

'Yes.'

'How much did you get for it?'

'One hundred twenty.'

'My cow was worth more than that.'

'It was not. Otherwise, I would have sold it for more than that. The broker is my friend and he did more haggling than I could expect anyone else to do.'

'Who was the broker?'

'Dirir.'

'Oh heavens! God in the heavens,' Ebla prayed.

'Yes. He is not a bad fellow.'

'You may be right.'

'What makes you happy?'

'Ebla,' her cousin addressed her for the first time since he came in.

'Yes?'

'Can we be alone for a little while?'

'Yes,' she said.

Ebla went to the widow's house. After she had gone her cousin whispered some private things to his wife.

'Are you sure it was the right thing?' asked his wife when he had finished talking.

He nodded. It was dark inside and naturally she could not see if he had nodded. She repeated the question.

'Yes,' he said aloud.

14

In the meantime, Ebla and the widow exchanged greetings. The widow had something to say, but since Awill was in the other room, she thought at first that she would not mention it. But then she changed her mind and told him to go down-town and buy her certain things. When he had gone, she said:

'Have you heard, Ebla?'

'No,' replied Ebla.

'You have not heard? Are you sure?'

'I don't know if I have. But what is it anyway?'

'That your cousin has given your hand to a broker?'

'No. I have not. Who told you?'

'I heard it from one of the man's relatives.'

'Is that the reason why he asked me to leave him and Aowralla to talk alone?'

'Is that why you came now?'

'Yes. He told me to leave them.'

'What about the fine?'

'A thousand shillings with a warning.'

'And did he say he had paid it?'

'I did not hear.'

'The broker paid him some money for your hand. As dowry or something.'

'Do you know the broker?'

'Yes.'

'Who is he?'

'He is sick. Very sick.'

'How sick?'

'They say he's got T.B.'

'Oh, has he?'

'Yes.'

'And what should I do?'

'I don't know, Ebla. I really don't know. I wish I knew what would be best for you.'

'But you are more experienced. You know better. What should I do? I must do something.'

It was the impulse of the moment that made her say this.

'Do you want to marry him?'

'No. I don't think I want to marry a sick man – especially one who is already sick.' And she told the widow why she had run away from the country. The widow kept quiet.

'What should I do?'

'I don't know.'

Ebla was paralysed in the region of the mind which gives one suggestions for things to do and paths to follow.

'Do you want to escape?' asked the widow.

'Where to?'

'Anywhere. Elope. Do something like that.'

'I don't know if I want to. I have had enough of that. Why? What is this about?'

'How old are you?'

'Nineteen or twenty. Why?'

'After one year, you will be a spinster.'

'Yes, I know.'

'Do you want to go to *Hamar*?'

'What would I do there?'

'You might get a husband.'

'I don't like this sort of marriage.'

'What do you mean?'

'I don't want to be sold like cattle.'

'But that is what we women are – just like cattle, properties of someone or other, either your parents or your husband.'

'We are human beings.'

'But our people don't realize it. What is the difference between a cow and yourself now? Your hand has been sold to a broker.'

'Just like Bafto. He has sold it too.'

'Did he sell that cow?'

'Yes. This morning. And he was speaking about a certain broker whom he met this morning. Or did he say that this broker sold it for him at a high price?'

'But what will you do?'

'I won't marry a broker. Unless I choose him, I cannot think of anything else to do. Maybe something will come up.' With this said, Ebla left the widow.

When Ebla returned to her cousin's house, Aowralla said that she had been waiting for her.

'Why?'

She told Ebla that her husband had brought her some new clothes.

'Should I or should I not accept?' Ebla asked herself.

She took the bundle and immediately examined the contents. Inside was a six-metre sheet of a new type of dress she had never worn, but had always wanted to own. On it, some animals were painted. Normally on this type of dress one would find butterflies, swans, and even eagles. However, this one had hedgehogs on it, raising their heads as if they wanted to smell the wearer or curling up themselves into a bundle as if waiting for an ambush.

'What is this for?'

'I don't know much about it.'

'He did not say anything?'

'No. Not much.'

'What are the little things that he said?'
'Wait for him.'
'I will see him only tomorrow.'
'Yes. Then wait till tomorrow.'
'I will.'
'I have got thirty-six days, during which I should remain locked in the house. But when I have finished my convalescent period, then you won't find much to do.'
'You mean in the house?'
Aowralla nodded.
'What is the name of the broker?'
'Who?'
'The broker.'
'Why?'
'I just want to know. He helped my cousin.'
'Dirir, that's his name.'
After a while, Ebla said she would go out for a walk.
'Where to?'
'Maybe to the widow's.'
'I will sleep. I am tired and hungry. The kid has been sucking me and I am empty inside.'
'Do you want anything to eat?'
'No. Don't bother.'
'If you are hungry, I can make you something.'
'I don't have the tongue to eat with: it is heavy. Sleep will do me good. Have you eaten?'
'No.'
'Why don't you prepare something for yourself?'
'When I was a kid, they used to tell us not to eat anything when you are given new clothes. You might spoil them.'
'But you are no longer a kid.'
'Just like a kid, I might dirty the new clothes.'
'Which you have not put on as yet!'

'Anyway, you sleep.'

'Blow out the lamp and take the box of matches with you. And when you come back, try not to disturb the baby.'

Ebla did as she was told, and she walked towards the widow's house.

15

On her way to the widow's house
(which Ebla now thought of as Awill's provisional home)
her legs seemed to betray her. Her lips moved rapidly while
she wondered about the present situation and what it
might lead to. She had escaped before: it was no longer an
enigma – the only problem was where to go.

Ebla was afraid of the fact that she might not be able to
summon the required courage to talk to Awill. 'What should
I say to him? I hardly know him. And people don't think
highly of a girl who asks a man to marry her. But why should
one marry after all? To beget children? To raise a quiver-
full of children? Only that? Or is it to love also? To love a
man? In the history of love in Somaliland the most fascinating love story occurred somewhere near Barbara between
Hodan and Elmi Bowderi. He died of love. Was it worth it?
What happened to Hodan? I wish I knew. I wish I could
meet her. Maybe she has lots and lots of interesting stories
to tell me.'

Ebla leaned against the main door and continued her
train of thought. There were a couple of people going
nearby with a flash light. She could see the light, but it was
only a lamp to Ebla.

She knew love was out of the question, as far as her case
was concerned. Awill did not love her. How could he love
her? He had met her only once. She did not know if there
was such a thing called 'Love', which could exist between a
person like Awill and herself. Enslavement was what

existed between the married couples she had met. The woman was a slave. And she was willing to be what she had been reduced to, she was not raising a finger to stop it. But since she would not be able to do anything about it, why not marry simply for the sake of living a married life and thus avoiding spinsterhood? In the process she would live to be a married woman. Why not get married to Awill – or whoever falls into the ditch of matrimony, she chuckled to herself – in order to get children of her own blood, of her own stock? They would be her own babies, which would be nice. She loved children. She loved Aowralla's child, so long as she did not think of it as her cousin's; but she must overcome this sudden bitterness, she thought to herself.

From experience she knew that girls were materials, just like objects, or items on the shelf of a shop. They were sold and bought as shepherds sold their goats at market-places, or shop-owners sold the goods to their customers. To a shop-keeper what was the difference between a girl and his goods? Nothing, absolutely nothing.

What an agony, what a revolting situation! Naturally women are born in nine months (unless the case is abnormal) just like men. What makes women so inferior to men? Why is it a must that a girl should refund a token amount to her parents in the form of a dowry, while the boy needs the amount or more to get a woman? Why is it only the sons in the family who are counted? For sure this world is a man's – it is his dominion. It is his and is going to be his as long as women are oppressed, as long as women are sold and bought like camels, as long as this remains the system of life. Nature is against women.

If a woman wants to argue about her fundamental rights not being fulfilled by her husband, it is always a man that she must see – at the government office and every other place (she smiled to herself for being conversant with the town terminologies). Before she has opened her mouth, she is condemned to the grave. Aren't men the law?

'But it is good to sell yourself,' she told herself. 'Without a broker there is no bidder – and no auctioneer. All I need is the Sheikh's fee if Awill wants to marry me.

'Is it possible that the widow has spoken to him? Let us hope she has. Will I get a positive reply? Only God knows.

'But he is a man – like any other. But he may be different. In all probability he will be – otherwise I will try to reform him, to teach him, to break his pride, to turn him into a human being.'

On second thoughts she decided to go back and collect her new dress. 'That will help me in case we agree to elope together.' She tiptoed back. She timidly went in. Aowralla was awake.

'You have come back, have you?'

'Yes, but I will go out again. I want to show the new dress to the widow.'

'Come back soon.'

'I will.'

She walked into the widow's house, unalarmed, as she always was before. She found Awill reading a novel. He later told her that it was an Italian novel. It had a beautifully decorated cover, and Ebla, although she could not understand what it was about, was most impressed by it. But she could not endure looking at the semi-nude woman on the cover. She closed her eyes tight. She thought that this woman must have been photographed without her consent. It was a wicked work. Awill, sensing that there was somebody else in the room, raised his head from behind the novel. He saw Ebla. He was quite pleased and showed it.

'I heard,' he said.

'What?'

'That your cousin gave your hand to the broker this morning.'

'Who told you?'

'You know who. My aunt.'

Ebla pulled the new dress from beneath her arm and came forward.

'Is that a new dress?'

'Yes. I wanted to show it to her.' She thought, 'A dress for an excuse!'

'She is not far. She will be back.'

'Will she come back soon?'

He nodded.

He placed the novel beside him and sat on the edge of the bed. He then stood up. In the meantime, she took the seat.

'I am going back to Mogadiscio.'

'When?'

'Tomorrow.'

'How long will it be before you come back?' she asked, just to feel around.

'I don't know. Maybe a year. Do you want to come to Mogadiscio?'

'This is a bait. I must be cautious,' she thought.

'Yes. I would love to. They say it is a nice place, but full of wicked people. And everything is bad. And people smoke and do other evil things.' She thought, 'Are you like them, wicked?'

'There are some good people also.'

'Are there?' The question she wished to ask was 'Are *you* one?'

'Yes. As many as there are bad ones.'

'I have told you before that I don't know anybody there.'

'I have also told you that you know me.'

She kept silent, but betrayed her emotions by moving restlessly.

'Ebla.'

'Yes?'

'I want to know. . . ' and he left the sentence unfinished.

'What is it?'

'I have been trying to talk to you. Even before I heard about it. I wanted to marry a woman like you, but it was not possible. Something came up and we had to break off.'

'I know.'

'How?'

'Your aunt told me.'

'You know everything about me, do you?'

'Yes.' She thought, 'What a lie!'

'Can I say something?'

'Say it.' If he asked her, she would marry him.

'I want to marry you.'

Ebla hid her face in her hands. Her lips made some movements as though to speak, but she did not make any sound. She turned her back on him. She then lowered her eyes – pretending that the idea to marry him was something new to her. She wanted to say 'no'. To refuse as women do, even if they want it. She simply murmured.

Awill wanted to explain himself more fully, but she interrupted him. What she said was not only incomprehensible, but inaudible.

'Just say yes or no.'

'It is too much for me.' She thought, 'If only he would insist.'

'Say yes or no.'

'I cannot say,' she said, unable to face him. 'Go on insisting' she thought.

'You cannot say either?'

'Yes.'

87

'What yes?'

'Yes.' She wished he wouldn't push her too hard, after all she could still say no.

'I request you. Just say yes or no.'

She nodded. If she actually *said* yes perhaps it would cheapen her in his eyes.

Awill was very glad that she had decided to marry him. He found a new soul within himself. He looked himself up and down. He looked at his surroundings. Then he looked her in the eyes. She lowered her head.

He asked her to come nearer.

She did so but covered her face with the cloth she had. He told her to uncover her face. She did. He told her to sit on the edge of the bed, and she did this too. But when he came nearer to kiss her she resisted, for this was a completely new experience for her. She said in a shrill voice, 'Don't. Don't. I don't want you to touch me. Let us talk and talk till morning, but I don't want your body to come nearer to mine. We ought to be separate and not stay in this room. After we reach Mogadiscio and have the Sheikh pass our engagement I am willing to do . . . '

'All right. Let us reach Mogadiscio.'

The widow came in. She was surprised to find Ebla there. Awill quite happily (and proudly) told the widow that he and Ebla had agreed to elope together the next morning.

'I am very happy,' said the widow. 'Come Ebla. Come with me. Let us women do a little bit of talking,' she said, extending her finger to Ebla, who caught it gently and followed her into the room.

That night, they did a little bit of talking. The widow told her many things about life and men. From experience.

Part Three

*Why do I ever think
of things falling apart?
Were they ever whole?*

Arthur Miller: *After the Fall*

16

In Mogadiscio, Awill took Ebla

to his single rented room somewhere in Bondere, the biggest zone in the city. Ebla felt more tired than she ever had. Never in her life had she ever felt so broken and exhausted. Her legs were asleep when she alighted from the bus. She had rubbed them hard on the warm bus-seat and life returned to them. The bus was very uncomfortable, for the journey took over eight hours, with only one break at Bula Burte. The heat was unbearable – the seat where she was became quite wet under her. Several times, she moved a little bit towards Awill when her underneath became extremely warm.

In the bus Ebla and Awill hardly spoke. Awill tried to make her talk, but he failed. She seemed to enjoy silence.

Seeing that she was in a state of dizziness, Awill asked her if she would like to stretch herself on the only bed in the room. Apart from the bed, there were only books and a wooden box underneath the bed, and dirty trousers and shirts scattered all over the place.

'I will sleep for a while. But what will you do?' said Ebla, putting the luggage on one of the chairs.

'I will take a bath and read for a while.'

'I cannot sleep like that.'

'What do you mean?'

'With you inside, how can I sleep?'

'Do you want me to remove myself?' he asked. Ebla nodded.

'Well, I won't come in. But I guess I should be allowed to take a nice bath.' It was about five in the afternoon.

Ebla opened her eyes and found Awill sitting on the chair reading a book.

'Did you have a good sleep?' he asked her.

'Remarkable,' she replied.

She had not seen him smoke until this time and it never occurred to her that he might. So when she saw smoke climbing into the air, she thought that something was burning.

'Is something burning?'

'Why?' he asked innocently.

'I see smoke coming from below.'

'Oh. This,' he said showing his cigarette. He pulled at it and puffed a heavy ring of smoke into the air. Ebla closed her eyes. She was quite upset about it.

'Why didn't you tell me you smoked?' she said.

'Why?'

'Because I would never have accepted to marry you.'

'But I smoke.'

'I see that only now.'

'I don't smoke heavily.'

'What will I say to my people.'

'About my smoking?'

'Yes.'

'Well, it is nobody's concern. I smoke because I like to smoke. What has that got to do with it?'

Ebla always heard that many men in the towns smoke, but women rarely smoke, unless they are harlots – and they did it to attract the attention of their would-be clients.

Funnily enough, it reminded Ebla of a story she had heard several times. It is said that a man from the country went to Hargeisa to sell some cows. After he had sold them, he decided to go to the mosque and say his prayers. On the

way he saw a man sitting smoking somewhere on the pavement. He approached the man and asked him if he would be
willing to keep his money for him until he came back from
the mosque. When the smoker agreed, he handed over his
money. The man from the country went off to the mosque,
said his prayers and came back to collect his money from the
man with the fire in his mouth. Somewhere in the area, he
met a man smoking.

'Give me my money,' he said to this man.

'What money?' They started to fight and the police
eventually intervened.

'How do you know that it was him that you gave your
money to?' the police asked the countryman.

'Because he had a fire in his mouth.'

Ebla thought that the man from the country was not a
good example, and she dismissed the story from her mind.
But only God knows if this is a true story.

Ebla looked in the direction of Awill. He was engrossed
with his reading. The silence was intense and all she could
hear was his breathing.

Ebla then caught sight of an unwashed glass and the tea-
leaves in it attracted her attention. 'He must have drunk tea
from the glass the last time he was here,' she thought. Again
this reminded her of an incident she called the sugar-
incident. The story goes that a certain tribe had a sackful of
sugar: it was the first time they had ever got the chance to
own so much of this sweet thing. One by one they came and
tasted it; they found it quite sweet. The time of distribution
came, but everyone wanted to have more of it. There was
not enough and a riot began somewhere in the dwelling.
Two men had such a big squabble that the old men of the
dwelling had to come in to put an end to the fight. The
suggestions of the old men were listened to one after the
other. They could not solve anything. After a long time, an

old man put forward a suggestion that the sugar should be poured into the common river, which would then become sweet. The idea was acceptable to everyone, and so they dumped the sugar into the river.

Ebla heard that the townspeople thought that the country-people had done an unwise thing. 'But,' she thought to herself, 'The old man only wanted to bring the squabble to an end: he was wise. But they are only townspeople and they don't understand. And even if they do they ignore it.'

Ebla lisped through her teeth.

Awill had stood up.

'Where are you going?' she asked him.

'Not very far. I want to ask my landlady to prepare dinner for us tonight.'

'Yes. But I want to cook. I can cook.'

'I don't have the cooking utensils. I don't eat here. Only occasionally I make tea.'

He left her and came back after a while. She was still lying on the bed. He stood near the bed and said, 'Yes. She said that some guests of hers have cancelled their dinner. We can have it. Her maid will bring us something to eat.' At about seven in the evening, dinner was served.

17

When they had had their dinner,
Ebla wanted to know where she was to sleep for the night.

'Here,' said Awill.

'Where?' asked Ebla.

'Of course here. Where else?'

'What about you?'

'Here.'

'What about beds?'

'On the same bed.'

'But I can't.'

'Why?'

'Because I can't.'

'Why?'

Ebla sat up in bed. She never expected such a trick to take place. She saw that the door had been bolted on the inside. Awill had already stood up. Ebla became frightened.

'But we are not married,' she protested.

'Yes we are.'

'How?'

'Why did you come with me from Belet Wene?'

'Of course to marry you.'

'Then we *are* married.'

Awill went towards the door to check if he had bolted it properly. Ebla lay terrified on the bed, her elbows underneath her belly, raising her head a little bit to have a better view of what Awill was doing.

Awill came back and sat on the edge of the bed. With his

back turned to her, he unknotted his shoe-laces, then pulled off his socks, which, Ebla noticed, now stank badly.

'You are my wife,' he said.

'You don't come near me,' she retorted.

'I said you are my wife.'

He moved towards her. Her feet were under his arms, and his face near her breasts. He crawled upward, towards her, like a crocodile. He was fully dressed and so was she. He wanted to kiss her, but he checked himself. He knew that it was uncommon in the country, and that she would not be familiar with it. She had never been kissed, he guessed.

He caught her by the arms, and whispered as if to hypnotize her: 'You are my wife.'

Ebla wanted to get out of bed and run away. For a second she forgot that the door was bolted and that it would take her some time before she was able to unbolt it. She also forgot that Awill was in her way. It was not that he was stronger than she, but a woman never fought with a man, she should be submissive and never return his blows. A good woman should not even cry aloud when her husband beat her. 'But this is not my husband – not yet. Maybe later. Maybe, when I have become his wife, he can do whatever he wants with me and I won't cry,' she thought.

Ebla's attempt at jumping over him and running away was not successful. And the more she tried to free herself, the better chance she gave him of getting hold of her.

Awill stood up straight and showered hard blows upon Ebla – in the mouth, at her head, on her belly. He gave her a kick or two on the belly as she tried to bite him. Ebla did not cry, she wanted to, but she knew she should not. Awill grasped her by the plaited hair and pulled her down. Now he jumped over her and sat upon her belly, her body heaving underneath his.

'You are my wife.'

96

'When I have become your wife, I will accept everything. But this is rape. Do you want to rape me?' she asked.

'No. You are my wife.'

They were both calm now. And Awill thought that he had better talk her to bed. He might succeed, he thought.

'Look. It is only a matter of hours.'

'What?'

'When we shall see the Sheikh.'

'But we can't do anything until our engagement has come through.'

'I know. But we are going to get married, aren't we? We surely are. So it comes to the same thing.'

After a while, Awill lay beside her on the bed. He expected her to move, but she did not. He made several passes at her and touched her head. Although unpermitted, Awill went over to blow out the lamp. Then he undressed.

Now that they were in bed and it was dark, she did not object to his passes. He moved towards her, groaned, and made some whispering sounds, as if he were telling her the secrets of a life he had lived through. He unknotted her dress and she raised no objections: she only moaned. He touched her head again.

'Did I hit you hard?'

'No.'

Ebla was very frightened, not of Awill, but because she was a virgin. She had heard lots of women talking about the pain one undergoes when one has one's first sexual intercourse. She had been circumcised when she was eight: the clitoris had been cut and stitched.

She wished more than anything else that she was not a woman. She remembered Aowralla's painful child-delivery when she was in Belet Wene. That was a recent occurrence, but she recalled many other incidents, both similar and dissimilar, and all this scared her out of her wits.

If a woman slept with a man, her relations either shot her or knifed her to death. It had happened quite a number of times in the dwellings where she grew up. The dwellings consisted of a small number of huts where people knew each other and where any woman with a man would be noticed. 'But this is Mogadiscio,' Ebla thought. 'And who would be able to know where one slept and whether a woman slept with a man? I wonder if anybody cares?'

Awill's naked body touched that of Elba. Awill was hot. Maybe because he had not satisfied his animal desires for days. It was a fortnight or so ago that he went to Shanganni, where the brothels are. He had paid the whore the amount she asked for, but when he was ready, she said she must just go out, but would come back in a minute or so. She went out and never returned. He had gone to sleep. It was about four in the morning that he woke up to find himself in a whore's house. He hurriedly put on his trousers, fumbled for his shirt in the dark (he found it difficult to find the light switch) and went out. He had not been going to the whores for over a month before this. From that night on, he was determined never to visit a harlot's den again, no matter how sexually frustrated he might become. That was when he decided to marry.

He worked in the Ministry of Education as a clerk in the daytime and he taught in an evening school at nights. The evening school was meant for adults, and there he met some old women and some fairly young and gorgeous ones. He had dated one or two of his students, not to go to bed with, but just in order to have a woman around. One woman of about thirty-five with four children became very keen on him. At first he did not realize what the affair might lead to: he even went to her place two or three times and met her husband and her children.

Now and then he would visit her. Then one day the

woman and her husband had a big squabble and she ran away from him. The first night she took refuge in Awill's room. He had never shared a bed with a woman ten years his senior and now this gave him some sense of achievement.

'When do we call in the Sheikh?' Ebla was asking him now.

'Tomorrow.'

'Swear.'

'Upon the Great Allah.'

Ebla believed what he'd said; actually she mesmerized herself to believe it. Awill moved towards her slowly, placed his hand on her breasts and touched them. He then started to breathe fast and quick.

In a couple of hours and after a great deal of sweating he succeeded in breaking the virginity of Ebla. She moaned and groaned and bit the edge of her cloth. She closed her eyes so that the sweat would not go in, and tasted the sour sweat which dripped into her mouth. She bled a great deal.

18

Ebla wanted to vomit when she

woke up. She was no longer a virgin, she was a woman now,
the wife of Awill, but only if he wanted her. Awill was
still asleep. She stretched out her arms to touch him, she
swallowed hard to summon up her courage to touch him.
She pulled his sheet and he woke up.

'Are you awake?' she asked.

'Yes.'

'Go and call the Sheikh,' she ordered timidly.

'Not now.'

'When, if not now?'

'Later. When people have woken up.'

Ebla kept silent.

'Go and make us some tea,' he said.

'I cannot move. I cannot go out.' She thought, 'you have
almost cut my intestines to pieces.'

'I cannot move out either. I am terribly exhausted. Usually
one drinks milk and tea on such occasions.'

'I don't want any.' The only thing *she* wanted was a
Sheikh to solemnize their wedding.

Ebla slept again. Awill looked at her. She had her eyes
closed and he could see that she was a very lovely creature.
He admired her thick eyebrows and her eyes looked quite
lovely when they were closed. Awill soon fell asleep again
too.

He woke up when he heard a knock on the door.

'Who could it be?' he asked himself.

'Who is it?' he said aloud.

There was no answer, but the knocking continued. He got out of bed, and searched for his heel-less slippers which he had not used for a long time, found the pair underneath the bed and went towards the door to open it. He stopped and turned back. He covered Ebla with the bed-cover in case the person turned out to be a nuisance.

'Who is it?' he said again, when he was a few inches away from the door.

'Open,' said a woman's voice.

Although Awill could not place whose voice it was, he opened the door. He found his landlady.

'Good morning,' she said.

'Good morning,' he replied.

'How is she?'

'Fine.'

'Asleep?'

Awill kept silent. In the meantime Ebla came back from the black sleep which she had been imposing upon herself.

'Do you want anything?' the landlady asked Awill.

'We want breakfast,' Awill said.

'I have made it for you.'

'Good.'

'What else?'

'I want a Sheikh. And two witnesses. They should both be men, unknown to myself. Naturally, Ebla would not have met them.'

'Ebla is her name?'

'Yes.'

'How old is she?'

'I don't know. I never bothered to ask her.'

'Yes. I will call the Sheikh and two male witnesses.'

'And you can ask the maid to bring us the breakfast as soon as Ebla wakes up. I am famished and so is she.'

'You let me know when she wakes up.'

'I will call you.'

'Do that.'

Ebla could feel that he was bolting the door on the inside although she still had her eyes closed. Awill had no idea that she had heard what had been said. He quite softly climbed into the bed lest he should disturb Ebla. Ebla pretended to be asleep, and he followed suit.

All of a sudden she wanted to do a bunk. 'How could one wait to undergo the same pain again,' she thought. Last night it had been extremely painful. Inside her, she felt sure that copulation was nothing but getting children. She wondered if she wanted children. If she had to go through the torture of the previous night again – or the agony which she felt when she nursed Aowralla – then she certainly did not want any.

Now more than anything, she wanted to visit the lavatory, but she could not move. Her joints ached and, with her glands swollen, she could not possibly move. Whenever she opened her eyes, she saw Awill. She felt some sort of mental anguish, but naturally her bodily aches would not last long, she thought.

She had never been as grateful to her mother – and grandmother and great-grandmother, for that matter – as she felt at this particular moment. This was only the beginning. She regretted that her mother had died before she could pay tribute to her. As might be expected, she did not now feel sorry about leaving her grandfather helpless. He was a man – just like any other man. What was the difference? His wife (her grandmother) must have suffered under his brutal manhandlings.

She felt morbid and weak. Awill had covered her head and he could not imagine what she looked like underneath. She was hungry, but she did not have the energy to eat. Her head was whirling, her teeth and tongue tasted as if she hadn't brushed them for ages. Putting out her tongue a little bit, she could see a film of white scum in the middle of it and could feel the red layer below, but her eyes ached when she did this.

She touched her hair. The strands of the plait were still there. Only an unmarried woman – and especially a virgin – could keep it plaited. She was certain she was not a virgin, but was she married? There was a promise, but that was all there had been so far.

She nervously began to unplait her hair. The hair came down to her shoulders. She remembered the time when she was quite young, about eight or nine. At that time, they would shave the whole head leaving only a knot on the skull. They had continued to shave her hair until she was fourteen. Then she was considered a grown-up girl, her hair was allowed to grow and plaited for her. When she was seventeen, she could plait the hair of another girl and get hers done for her by the same girl – an exchange arrangement.

This plaiting had been done by one of her friends in the country, who was always spoken of as the best one at plaiting. The interlacing of hair was so well done that Ebla found it difficult to undo all by herself. She sat up and again nervously pulled the hair apart. She had oiled it a week or so ago. The hair was quite dark, wavy and she had a handful of curls on the nape. In towns, they cut this type of hair. The pulling and undoing of hair woke Awill up.

'What are you doing?' he said.

'Nothing.'

Ebla had put her hands on her thighs before he could see them.

'I dreamt of an earthquake.'

'I did not feel it,' she said humorously.

'How could you? Anyway, are you hungry?'

'Yes,' she said.

Awill got out of bed, stood at the door and shouted to the landlady.

'Aunt Asha.'

A woman's voice replied, 'Yes. I will come straight away. I have it ready.'

And after a little while, a lady in her late forties, who could easily be mistaken for a rich woman, came in. She was in an expensive dress, had her eyebrows darkened with coal ground for the purpose, and walked haughtily. She had a double chin, and the one below quivered whenever she spoke. She was hefty and the floor, which badly needed repairing, moved up and down under her weight. Her buttocks were stretched backward and her belly forward, as if she were pregnant, but Ebla thought that she was not the type to get pregnant. She held the china plate in her hands.

'Here is breakfast for you,' she said.

She set down the plate on the chair, then glanced at Ebla who had lowered her eyes.

'Is the Sheikh coming?' asked Awill.

'Yes.'

'When?'

'Very soon.'

She did not say more, but left and closed the door behind her.

'She is a helpful woman,' said Awill.

'You know her better,' Ebla retorted. All this time Awill had been walking to and fro. He again went to the door and bolted it.

'Come. Eat,' said Awill.

'I cannot. I'm not hungry.'

'But you said you were.'

'I no longer am. I don't feel hungry.'

'Well, if you don't want to eat, I am going to. Surely your stomach will tell you later when you feel hungry. Are you sure you are not hungry?' Ebla nodded.

It was not so much lack of appetite that prevented her from eating, but the pain she felt in every joint of her body. Like everybody else, she wished she could be what she wasn't. She knew she was catching at a straw, wishing for the impossible. What she wished was that she could be somebody else, either an old woman, so that she could look back on this day as one in a long forgotten past; or a man, so that she would not have to worry about it.

She could sense the movement of Awill's jaws and the sound of his swallowing – just like a cow eating fodder. She was hungry, her stomach was turning over, empty, waiting to be filled. 'My jaws have not been used for over twelve hours and they will go rusty.' she thought. 'But I cannot eat. I cannot. I just cannot eat.'

Awill had finished eating the oiled bread and drunk his tea. He wiped his hands on his robe and came forward. From his eyes she could tell what he was after.

'No. You cannot do that.'

'Why not?'

'Not now. Some other time.'

To Ebla, Awill was a bad example of the male sex. He acted more like a donkey, as far as the satisfaction of his animal desires were concerned. 'Copulation is a means of getting children,' she thought. 'But this is not the only thing that a man shares with his woman. Donkeys, and all irrational animals for that matter, get to satisfy their desires, and prefer it to anything else. But even these animals prefer some seasons to others. Men should consider that the existence of a woman is not just a means to an end, but that she can be an indispensable companion for life. I could be bought, I could be sold, just in the way that my cousin tried to sell me

– or my first would-be husband bought me. But one thing they could not pay for is my indispensability. I am a woman. And I am indispensable to man.'

Meanwhile, they heard a knock on the door.

'Who is it?' Awill shouted.

'Asha.'

'Yes. I am coming.'

'The Sheikh is at the door.'

Awill opened the door. In the clearing, they could see a Sheikh, with a beard painted with henna and two other young Sheikhs.

'Do you want them in here?' Asha asked.

'No. Let us go to your room.'

'What about her?'

'I will ask the Sheikh to go and ask her to name him as her agent to speak for her.'

Awill went over and spoke to the Sheikh.

The Sheikh had a weary-looking face. He was about fifty, quite tall and handsome. The others were comparatively short and young and did not utter a single word. Maybe they were silent because they were only witnesses.

'I will carry back her *wilaya*,' the Sheikh said and entered the room where Ebla was lying.

'*Nabad*,' said the Sheikh.

'*Nabad*,' Ebla replied, sitting up in bed, wracked with pain. She tried not to show her condition.

'What is your name?'

'Ebla.'

'And your father's?'

'Qorrah.'

'Are you willing to marry Awill. . . . ?'

'Yes.'

'What about the *Yered*?'

'Nothing.'

'What is your *Meherr*?'

'Whatever he is willing to pay.'

Ebla wanted to enquire if she had made a mistake by sleeping with Awill before they got married, but she could not bring herself to ask this.

The Sheikh left her, then a few minutes later the whole group came back. The Sheikh told her that he had made the answers as she had told him and Awill and she were now husband and wife.

19

Ebla was quite delighted to think
of herself as a wife. It really did not matter whose wife,
because it all came to one thing: that she had got married.
Looking back on her escapades, she did not find them very
fruitful. She had made many mistakes, from which she learnt
things that she ought to have known before.

She struggled with her plaits again and pulled them apart.
This hurt her, especially at the roots of her hair. She had
undone several when Awill came to satisfy the animal desire
in him.

Being the second time, it was painful, but not as bad as the
first time. As soon as they had finished, there was a knock on
the door. Awill went to open it.

'Your friend Jama is here,' said Asha.

'Where is he?'

'Should I call him?'

'Yes.'

Jama emerged from behind Asha whose huge body had
been hiding him.

'Jama, come on in.'

Jama came in after shaking hands with Awill, and Asha
went away.

'I am married, Jama,' said Awill, as if Ebla were deaf or
were not present. Ebla had covered herself with the bed-
spread, and was in no mood to greet a stranger. She still felt
the pain, which lingered in her loins. It seemed now that the

pain was leaving the lower part of her body first. She felt warm inside and tried to breathe less, so that under the cover, she would not swelter.

'How are you, Jama?'

'I am fine, thank you,' replied Awill's friend.

Ebla uncovered her head and she could see Jama clearly. Jama had his back turned and she could inspect him without him knowing. He was thin and short and had his hair parted on the left side. He quite badly needed a shave. But maybe this was the way people did things in Mogadiscio, Ebla thought. 'They really do things awkwardly and then boast about it afterwards. If only they knew how ridiculous they are,' she thought.

'How is the Ministry?' asked Awill.

'Fine,' responded Jama.

'No changes anywhere?'

'No.'

'How about you?' Awill continued.

'I am still in the same office.'

'Any newcomers?'

'Yes.'

'Who?'

'A girl.'

'Where does she work?'

'The same office as you were in.'

Awill looked back to see if Ebla was listening to what was being said between them. But she was quicker and had already hidden beneath the sheet again.

'You see, she has actually taken over your place.'

'But I am coming back soon. I have only five more days before my vacation ends.'

'I know,' said Jama and kept quiet.

'Do they have a new job for me?'

'No.'

'Then what happens? Am I sacked? I know the people at the personnel office are up to some nasty tricks. Tell me the truth.'

'You are not sacked. Far from it.'

'Then what?'

'You are to fly to Italy in another week's time. I brought a letter to you from the Ministry. That is why I came. I did not know that you had got married or anything. I came yesterday, but the room was locked. By sheer luck, I came back today and here I find you, strange, isn't it? So you are married, you are lucky. Isn't it fabulous?'

'The wedding?'

'Yes.'

'*Ma voglie andare in Italia?*' said Awill in Italian.

'Whatever you think best,' said Jama in Somali.

'*Ho mia moglie. Ma non voglio distruggiare la mia vita per una donna,*' Awill continued in Italian.

'Whatever you say,' said Jama in Somali.

Ebla, although listening, could not work out what had been said. She had never learnt any foreign language, except Arabic, which she always thought of as the language of the Koran.

'When do they want us to go?'

'In a week's time. Haven't you got everything ready – passport, vaccination, and so on?'

'Not the vaccination, but everything else.'

'Good. They want you people to come back in three months. They have changed all the programmes. There are twelve of you. You will go on a study tour to Italy and visit some of the schools to give you an idea how to run them when you are appointed heads of schools here. You will come home one month before Independence.'

'That will be quite splendid.'

'Yes, it will be especially good once you have come back

and taken over the schools from the bastard Italians. Independence will bring about new life in the minds of everybody. We shall prosper and the Gentiles will perish.'

'I am longing for it. I hope I won't die before Independence Day.'

To Ebla, this did not mean much. The widow had tried to explain certain things, of which this was one. The word was now familiar to her. How could a man accept orders from another? She had never met a foreigner in her life, either black or white, other than one *Amhar*. So at this point, she became disinterested in what they were talking about and resumed undoing her hair.

'But what were they saying when they were speaking the language I could not understand? What was that language? Maybe it is one of their languages they speak in towns or places like Mogadiscio,' she thought.

When Ebla tried to eavesdrop on what her husband and Jama were saying to each other, she saw the latter on his feet again. He said he must go.

'I am sorry I could not offer you something to drink. You know my state of affairs, perhaps.'

'It does not matter.'

'When do you want to come again? I have five days more of my seven-day honeymoon.'

'Whenever I have time.' Jama said goodbye to Ebla and left.

'Who is he?' asked Ebla.

'A colleague in the office.'

'Why did he come?'

'Because he had something to pass along to me,' said Awill. 'Oh, he forgot to give me the letter,' continued Awill, as if speaking to himself.

They heard a rapping on the door, which Awill answered.

'I am sorry. I forgot to give you the letter,' Jama said. He fumbled in his pocket for the letter, fished it out and handed it to Awill. 'I am going now. 'Bye,' said Jama.

Awill tore open the letter and read all the information concerning his departure and everything. 'Eight days from now you will have to be in Rome,' the letter said.

He knew what to do about Ebla with regard to this departure. He had decided even before he arrived in Mogadiscio.

20

Six days had passed by,

unnoticed They flew like a beautiful bird that one knows will
never return. The bird flies by, ruffling up its feathers, and
dropping some gorgeous-looking ones. Each day passed in a
similar manner, and Ebla was quite delighted with the way
things were. Asha either attended to their wants or sent in
someone to do it for them. Ebla affected ignorance and never
discussed Awill's departure for Italy with him. She accepted
the situation with no resentment. It was part of a man's life
to travel for the benefit of the family.

In a way, she was very thankful to the Almighty that he
was not going to a tribal war, and that there was no need for
her to worry about it. He was going elsewhere. 'His work
in that place, whatever its name is, will benefit us,' she
thought. 'But in a tribal war, one never knows who will
come back in one piece and who won't.' It all depended upon
how each man fought, or really, to be more accurate, it
depended upon fate.

Ebla recalled many girls of her age-group, sometimes
younger than her and sometimes older, whose young
uncultivated husbands had been slaughtered, and who had
thus gained great 'prestige.' She was not acquainted with the
external world, however, and Italy sounded very unfamiliar.
'Maybe it is the place which the widow spoke to me about,
the white man's land.'

It was about nine in the morning. Awill had just got up
and was taking a shower before he went out after seven days'

imprisonment in the house. Only a couple of people had called on them. Jama had come three times, the third time he brought along another friend and Ebla spoke to them that day. She felt a bit worried conversing with two strangers, two men, who were not courting her. It was Awill who asked her to talk to them. Jama's second visit had embarrassed him. Ebla had not opened her mouth, but had just listened to whatever they said, and had released some suppressed giggles once in a while. After he had gone, Awill said, 'Why did you not speak to him?'

'What should I say to him?' she asked.

'Anything. Say anything, but something. You think you are an Arab or somebody like that?'

'I would be happy if I were an Arab.'

'But you are not. So talk to people, or else cover yourself with a black veil, make two small holes for your eyes, and run away whenever a male friend comes.'

Ebla fully understood what her husband had told her that day, but she still wondered how she would be justified to talk with strangers.

In the meantime, Awill entered the room, wrapped in a robe, and drying his head with his towel. They looked at each other as if they had been arguing the whole morning. They did not seem to want to say anything to each other, and both remained silent.

Awill was the one to break the silence.

'I am going to Italy after two days.'

'I know.'

'Where is Italy, do you know?'

'The white man's land. Your aunt told me certain things about the people.'

'Well, I will go to that place.'

'For how long?'

'For three months.'

'And when will you leave?'

'I will fly after two days. Today is Friday. I will fly on Sunday.'

Ebla had no idea what he meant by 'I will fly', but she did not ask for an explanation, because she felt it was better to conceal her ignorance. To her, a bird could fly, but nothing else could. No planes had ever come her way, and maybe she would die before she embarked on one or flew in it. The first time she had ever travelled in a bus was when she was coming from Belet Wene. She had no intention of asking Awill how a bus worked. She had asked the widow how and she had said, 'I don't know. It has got many things tied to each other, and they go fast, like mad. But I don't have the knowledge to explain them to you.' Thus Ebla was in no mood to ask Awill about flying or anything of the sort.

'Don't you want to know what are the arrangements I am making for you during my absence?' he asked, with apparent condescension.

'It had never occurred to me that I would need anything during your absence. But now, come to think of it, what are the arrangements you have made?'

Awill by then had dashed over to the place where he had put his trousers and shirt a week ago. He had not used them for a week, as there was no need for him to put them on during the honeymoon week. He had robes on for all this time because they are more comfortable in the heat of Mogadiscio. He pulled on the trousers, though he wobbled as he did so and nearly fell on the chair.

Ebla had got out of bed too. Today she could walk properly. The only hindrance was that she could not face the bright sunlight which penetrated through the only window in the room. She kept her eyes partly closed. She walked barefooted, and stamped upon a black-beetle. She was walking aimlessly, perhaps to practise. Awill had by now got his shirt on.

'I will speak to Asha about a shop nearby where I can open an account for you.'

All this was new to Ebla. She could not follow what he had said, and again had no intention of asking for clarification. 'Perhaps Asha will explain it to me when he has gone,' she told herself. 'After three days he will have gone, won't he? Asha will explain. The widow has explained things; occasionally my cousin's wife Aowralla did, and now Asha will. Why shouldn't she? She seems to be a nice woman.'

'Do you follow me?' Awill asked her.

As if she woke up from a deep sleep, Ebla mumbled, 'Yes. Yes. I do.'

'If the shops say "no", then she will find you money to keep you going. She knows how much will be sufficient for you. Then I will send some money through Jama to you from time to time.'

Ebla did not follow what he was saying, but nevertheless she nodded her head.

Awill had gone out, she was left alone. Seven days. She had spent seven days in bed: the most comfortable seven days of her life but for the ephemeral pain of breaking her chastity. There she had slept by Awill's side. She had been served as if she were a queen, and her first and second days' bodily torture had been compensated. Rest, she had taken rest for seven days. Imagine! Seven whole days!

She was alone now. 'But my husband will come back. He will come back very soon, but after two days he will go to the white man's land. To travel is to learn, so we Somalis say. Then he will come home after 180 milking-instances.' (A day has two milking-instances, one in the morning and one in the evening. Those are the times when the beasts are milked.)

Ebla sat in the doorway. Somewhere to her left, she saw an

old razor-blade and picked it up. She turned around facing the inside of the room. She glanced round the room, then, with her legs stretched out and the wind ruffling her hair, she began cutting her nails. She had cut all the nails of the left hand and had just begun cutting her right hand, which she found a little bit more difficult, when she noticed the figure of someone, standing behind her. She turned and saw Asha.

'You don't cut your nails like that, nor do you throw them into the room. It is Friday, anyway, so you shouldn't cut them at all because it brings famine.'

'I did not know that,' said Ebla. 'Why this sudden unfriendliness,' she thought.

'Awill spoke to me about your bill. I have spoken to the shopkeeper, but he has refused. He has too many families taking goods on credit. So I will pay your bill until Awill has sent you some money from Italy.'

'*Ashantu*,' said Ebla.

As planned, Awill flew to Italy after two days. He left Ebla one day earlier than she expected and he did not even come home to say good-bye. Asha was quite unhappy about it, and later told Ebla so. After this, Ebla discovered many good things about Asha, which in a way pleased her.

Part Four

'Don't tamper
with Camarina'

A Sicilian Proverb

21

Ebla had no reason to object to
Asha's suggestion that they should cook and eat together,
which would lessen the expenses of both. To a certain extent,
it did. Ebla, little by little, learnt the background of Asha,
who she found was the most interesting character she had
met since she left the country. Aowralla had spent most of
the time in bed, and the widow was a widow – and widows
are normally uninteresting creatures (that is why their
husbands die before themselves, out of boredom).

But Asha moved around vigorously, which made life more
exciting. In the house, there were six rooms, built in the
style of a circular African type of hut, with little doors and
grass roofs, sloping to the sides. She rented the rooms to
different tenants, and only God knew how she collected the
rent from them. Perhaps that explained why she was so
business-minded, and spoke in such a terrifying tone. She
always had her elbows stretched out and had a sly smile on
her face. She had a black head-dress on, which she would
loosen deliberately. You could see curls of kinky hair,
greying on the forehead. Ebla could not help being fond
of Asha, because she was the first person who had ever
considered her her equal: she made Ebla aware of what
she was.

A week or so had passed when one day Jama turned up.
He said he had got a letter from Awill, who was in fine
health. Jama added that he had brought the letter with him.
He looked for the letter in his pocket and selected it out of

many. Ebla took the letter. Jama said it was not meant for her, but she could have a look at it.

Although she could not read anything she opened the envelope. In the envelope, there was a long letter which was only black strokes, stripes, lines, cross-wise lines and drawings, as far as she was concerned. But there was a photo; it showed Awill and another woman. The woman had nothing on except a swimming suit, her belly was showing and Awill's hand was resting on her breasts. It was the first time Ebla had held a photo in her hands. In the country, there was a belief that it shortened one's life to be photographed: you would die before you were due to. And even if she did not worry about this, she had never seen anyone with a camera to take her photo.

Jama thought that he had taken out the photo, but as soon as he realized he had made a mistake, he winced and looked away. He was just about to rush away when Asha appeared on the scene. Jama greeted her and said that he was just leaving, but would call on them some other time.

'You are leaving so soon? Why?' said Asha, who had no idea why he was in such a hurry.

'Yes. I will come back some other time.'

Ebla had the letter and the photo in her hand. She did not know what to do. She saw someone like her husband in a photo with a white woman, but anyone could perhaps convince her that they were not up to anything. If anyone had told her that that was the way things were done in the white man's land, she would have believed it. But she was furious; she was disappointed, not in Awill, nor in the white woman, but in herself. Things began to dawn on her, thoughts crowding in on her, unchecked.

'What is it?' inquired Asha.

'This,' said Ebla, and handed it to Asha.

Asha opened the letter, examined the photo, read the

letter with difficulty and bluffingly translated it into Somali for Ebla's understanding.

'What should I do?' Ebla asked and her voice was so serious that anyone could see that she needed help.

'I know what you should do,' said Asha.

'Tell me, then.'

'I will make us some tea. After that I will tell you what to do.'

It was about three in the afternoon. Ebla and Asha went to the latter's room, where Asha made the tea. There were many things that came to Ebla's mind, but she was determined about one thing: she would not run away. She had run from the country to a town, and from there to Mogadiscio. Now if she ran from Mogadiscio, she would run into the ocean. Ebla was not in the least prepared to take refuge in the ocean. 'Come what may, I am going to stick to Mogadiscio, until doomsday,' she thought.

Asha served the tea. Almost everybody in the place was away and it was very quiet.

'You see I have a suggestion to make,' Asha began. She gulped.

'I want to hear.' Ebla sipped the insipid tea.

'But will you listen?' Asha gulped again.

'Yes, I want to listen. I am very anxious to hear what you want to tell me; tell me everything. But don't please tell me to go back and escape again.' She took a mouthful of tea. It seemed to taste like a man to her.

'I have another suggestion.'

'Say it.' She took another mouthful of tea. It seemed to taste better; like a woman.

'Swear that you will do it.'

'I swear upon Allah. And may God kill my brother if I don't do it.'

Something rang in Ebla's mind. 'What could have

happened to my grandfather?' When she was in the country, she had sworn upon his death. Today it was not the case: she had said 'my brother'. 'What could happen to him? Well, that will be a problem for tomorrow. One at a time,' she thought, addressing the problems.

'There is a rich man whom I know. He came here several times to visit me. He saw you and asked me about you. I told him who you are, but I did not tell him that your husband is away. He asked me if I could approach you and talk to you.'

'What does he want?'

'I don't know, but I think he would accept whatever you say. He is very interested in you.'

'Do you know much about Islam?' Ebla suddenly asked, out of the blue, implying that Asha knew nothing.

'Very little. Why?'

'Well, you see, my cousin gave my hand to a man whom I never met. The Sheikh had pronounced my engagement to him. My cousin told me about it. That was why I eloped with Awill and came to Mogadiscio, but what does Islam say about my marriage to Awill? Is it legal?'

'I think . . . I don't know,' responded Asha.

'Is your rich friend married?' She didn't care if he was.

'Yes. With two daughters of marriageable age and two sons. He comes from Baidoa.'

'What is his name?'

'Tiffo.'

'What an awkward name. What does he look like? Is he quite old?' She delved into the life-history of the man.

'No, but he is rich.'

'Do you think he will marry me? I am eager for marriage any time – that was what Adan and Hawa started, but they were never married, were they?'

'I have no idea. But at first they say that brothers married sisters until there were enough women: men always out-numbered us.'

'When will he come?'

'Tonight. When he comes, I will tell him to come and talk to you. And I will ask the Sheikh and two witnesses to be ready in case he is willing. Today is Friday and there are some Sheikhs coming to recite the Koran in the house.'

'Do you think that will create any trouble for me after-wards?'

'It is a man's trouble. They will jump at each other's throats, but nobody will dare touch you.'

'Tell Tiffo that I am willing to marry him secretly. Maybe he will also want that. And if Awill comes back and doesn't want to return to me, then I will stay with him. I love life, and I love to be a wife. I don't care whose.'

'Yes, I will,' Asha assured her.

They finished their tea and adjourned their meeting. Ebla went to bed immediately after that and dreamed that her brother came. She also dreamed that her grandfather had died.

When she woke up, it was about seven in the evening. 'Tiffo has come,' Asha told her. Ebla washed her face with water and didn't use soap, which she still detested applying to her body. Then she changed into a new dress, which Asha had borrowed for the occasion from a neighbour.

22

Ebla repeated to herself that she
loved life. However, she did not really understand what life
was: she had a wrong interpretation of life. If her interpretation was right, then everybody's would be right. To her,
life meant freedom, freedom of every sort. 'One should
do whatever one wants to – that is life. That is what I love.'
Freedom: that was what she worshipped. Not the freedom
to sleep with any man, for every man was not worth sleeping
with, neither could every man be a good husband. She was
unique in forming ideas about things. Marriage was a sound
refuge. Probably nobody would get furious, she told herself.
She was afraid she might let herself down. Since she had not
seen Tiffo before, she thought he might be a ghost-like creature. But what would she do then? Run away. But where to?
No. No more escapades – not in the search for another man
anyway. If another man was in any way interested in her, he
could present himself. 'But that would be prostitution. No,
it would not be. I love life, and life lies in marriage, and
marriage is born out of a couple from opposite sexes.' (She
had not the slightest idea that there could be such people as
homosexuals.)

Ebla bunched her dress a little on the edges. She admired
the dress. Since she did not have a standing mirror she
strained her eyes to see her backside, tilting her neck. This
position made her feel a little bit giddy. She had just come
back to normality when Asha entered the room. Ebla asked
if he had accepted the proposition.

'Yes.'

'And the Sheikhs also?'

'The Sheikh is coming to see you in a short time.'

The process went just like that with Awill, except that she had no idea what this man looked like. The Sheikh came and asked the usual questions. 'What is your name? Your father's name? And are you willing to marry Tiffo?' She answered the questions. She placed her confidence in Asha and the Sheikh.

After some time, Tiffo came, unaccompanied. He was very short, had a brownish complexion and was fat. Ebla could hear him breathe. She thought it must be difficult for him to breathe. He entered the room, which was practically empty, with the exception of the bed on which Ebla slept. Asha had removed all Awill's clothes to her room earlier in the evening, when Ebla was taking a bath.

Now Ebla lay on the bed. Asha had instructed her not to uncover her face until she had been paid the *Waji Fur* fee by Tiffo. Tiffo sat on the bed and looked at the covered figure of Ebla. He tickled the soles of her feet and she tried not to laugh, suppressing her laughter.

'Uncover yourself,' said Tiffo, with a manly voice.

Ebla was frightened when she heard the voice. For a moment she was going to uncover her face, but she checked herself.

'The *Waji Fur* fee.'

'How much?' he asked.

'A hundred Somali shillings,' Ebla repeated the amount Asha had told her. 'But this is too much,' she told herself, and, had Tiffo not said, 'Here is the money,' she would have reduced the amount.

'Uncover your face; here is the money,' said Tiffo.

Ebla forgot that Asha had instructed her just to uncover a little of her face so that she could see if there was money.

She uncovered her face completely and Tiffo seized a piece of her cloth and dragged it towards himself. Strangely enough, he laughed and laughed and laughed, pulling Ebla's dress. Ebla stood aghast, her mouth open.

'You are beautiful,' he said, after laughing for a long time. 'Where do you come from?'

His language was a mixture of many dialects spoken in what is now known as the Somali Republic. Ebla could not follow what he said.

'Yes, what did you say?' she asked.

'You are not familiar with these Southern dialects?' he said in the common Somali.

'I don't know what you are talking about. What do you say?'

'Where do you come from?'

'Ogadenia.'

'Which part?'

'I don't know. Not far from Kallafo: do you know where it is?'

'Now it is in Ethiopia,' he said.

'Where is that?' she asked.

'Somewhere near your place,' he dismissed the subject.

He unlaced his shoes, and began undressing. He then stretched himself on the bed. His belly pounded up and down as he breathed; he loosened his belt.

'How long have you been in Mogadiscio?' he said.

'Over a month,' Ebla replied.

Ebla thought maybe this kind of going from one hand to another would come to an end one day. She never regretted doing anything. The suggestion to marry Tiffo was Asha's, the one to marry Awill was the widow's, the one to get engaged to an old man in the country (she had even forgotten his name now) was her grandfather's. It was always someone else's suggestions that she either accepted or rejected. One is fed with suggestions all through one's life, starting from the time one comes into this world and ending when one dies. 'Do this; do that; don't do this; don't do that,' – this is life. But it is a life that has been poisoned, the potion has been fed to us, like medicine. This is the medicine we live on, the medicine we eat and drink, but do we realize it?

She looked at Tiffo. He had fallen asleep and was snoring. 'He must have been tired,' she thought. From his features, she could see that he was a fool, although she could not explain what she saw. 'It must be money which he got illegally that fills his belly. Otherwise, why is it so big? She wished she could see what was inside; mashed potatoes and roots? People talked about machines in the stomach, which grind the food after we have eaten. They said that one had stomach-ache when something went wrong with the machine or it got tired or rotten. Constipation was the result of the bluntness of the grinding machine. which usually had teeth like pliers.

She noticed that Tiffo was opening his eyes little by little. He smiled sheepishly.

'How long have I been asleep?' he asked.

'Not for long,' she replied.

'Our marriage is secret.'

'I know.'

'Good. I pay you some money whenever I come. I don't know when I will. It all depends upon when I am in town. Sometimes, I will come late in the night. Sometimes I won't be able to sleep with you.'

'Why should it be a secret?'

'Do you dislike it?'

'It's not that I dislike it, but why must it be like this?'

'You see, I have a wife and two daughters of marriageable age. The daughters are in Mogadiscio: they study here. My small kids are with my wife in Baidoa, where she is the manager of my business. We are at odds and I want to divorce her, but not now.'

'I understand now.'

'Good. How old are you?'

'Nineteen.'

'My daughters are eighteen and sixteen.'

'Are they in Mogadiscio?'

'Yes.'

'Where do they stay? And who with?'

'With their aunt – maternal aunt. It is only trouble for me if anybody gets to know about my marriage to you.'

'But I am not too low for your dignity, am I?'

'No. You are a princess. Don't misunderstand what I say. I mean no harm.'

Tiffo stood up and said he would put off the light; he asked if there was anything she wanted before he put it off.

'No,' said Ebla.

On his way back to the bed, Ebla could hear the shuffling of his feet. She had no time to think any further: Tiffo was just like any other man, an animal, a beast, an untamed beast, but he could certainly talk a woman to bed.

Tiffo and Ebla lay side by side. His uncontrolled hands explored the valleys and prairies of Ebla's body on their own.

After the first go, he said,

'But you are not a virgin.'

'I am divorced,' explained Ebla.

'Asha did not tell me.'

'She did. It must have escaped you.'

'Well, it is better, much better. Who would ever want a virgin? Especially when he is my age!'

They jabbered away until late in the night. Early in the morning, he woke up and said he would go to Baidoa and might be back the following day.

23

Ebla woke up the next morning
and started worrying at once about the enigmatic situation that
had developed because of her acceptance of other people's
advice. Never for one single instant did she believe that she
was responsible for what she was doing. Others were
responsible – God was. 'It is according to His will, and the
fate that He has ascribed to me that things should go this
way.'

For breakfast, she went to Asha's room. Asha, who had
just woken up, looked fatter than ever.

'How was he?' was the question Asha put to her.

'I don't know much about men. I have met only two men,
but Awill is better.'

'How?'

'I cannot explain.'

'What about the *Waji Fur*?'

'He played a trick on me.'

'But I told you that he would.'

'Anyway, he did, and that is what counts: no fee.'

Asha was no longer interested. Her main interest lay in
money; it circulated in her blood. And in no time, she had
become more furious than Ebla had ever seen her. She
shouted at some of the tenants of her house.

'Don't break that door. The hinges are broken. Why did
you do that?' she rebuked an old woman, who occupied one
of the rooms.

To a kid, who was playing with water, she said, 'Don't

splash water around. We cannot afford to waste water. Where is your mother?'

'There,' he replied. She called to his mother and told her to stop the kid playing around like that.

Ebla was uncertain what was the cause of all this upheaval. She thought that it was money that controlled the nerves of Asha, made her pleased with the world, or infuriated her. She postponed her idea of going to her room to get her some money from what Tiffo had given her the previous night. This was not as *Waji Fur*, but to buy some clothes and food.

'Shall I make us some tea?' she suggested to Asha, as the latter took the stool near her, finishing her scolding.

'Yes. That will do you good.'

'And shall I buy some bread from the woman next door?'

'Do you have money?'

'Yes, some.'

'Do then,' Asha said, cutting the conversation short.

When they had had their breakfast, Jama came. Ebla and Asha were sitting together, not speaking to each other. The empty glasses from which they had drunk their tea were near Ebla. When she saw Jama, she tried to adjust herself: she had not washed her face. She had thought that she did not care what anybody thought of her, but now she realized that she cared what she thought of herself with regard to others.

'I wish I had my photo taken with Tiffo last night to prove something to Jama. But he is only a friend, a poor friend. He is not responsible for someone's else's actions. Nobody is,' Ebla thought when she saw Jama.

'*Nabad*,' he greeted them.

'*Nabad*,' they both said.

'I thought I might see you before I went to work. I got something from Awill,' said Jama.

'Another photo?' said Asha sarcastically.

'No.'

'What then?' asked Ebla.

'Money,' he said.

'How much?' Asha wanted to know.

'Three hundred Somali shillings.'

Asha stood up and put her hand on his shoulder, but, in doing so, accidentally touched his breast pocket, so that it seemed as though she were trying to put her hand into his pocket and take the money out.

'You are another *Khadar*, an agent of the Prophet *Khadar*, you are. Take it from me,' said Asha.

'Shall I give you the money?' Jama enquired of them.

'Yes,' said Asha. 'Give it to me. Give it to me.' Jama looked in the direction of Ebla. Ebla nodded her approval, and smiled. Asha had her hand stretched out to receive the money. She was all smiles.

Jama told them that Awill would be returning a little earlier than had been planned before. And he departed saying that he would try to call upon them any time he heard from Awill.

Ebla's attempt to brush aside anything which might remind her of Awill, made her think about her grandfather and young brother. For certain, she did not regret walking out on Awill: he had done the same to her, she reasoned with herself. He started it: 'A nose for a nose, an ear for an ear, that is what the Koran says,' she reminded herself.

'What could have happened to Grandfather the day I left?' She could not guess what could have happened to him.

She looked around her and discovered that Asha had gone away.

She was too dog-tired to stand, too thoughtless to think, too tired to move, too disgusted to do anything.

She thought she had heard a stampede. She wanted to raise her head and see what was happening, but she closed her eyes in weariness. For one second, she thought the whole world – beasts, human animals and oceans, buildings – was stampeding and would crush her into pieces. For one second a psychiatrist would have considered her case a dangerous one. She hung somewhere between the seven seas and the seven hills and the eight heavens.

Her head whirled, but she shook it. All she had experienced was an imaginative fear, a day-dream in which she was still awake, seated somewhere in Mogadiscio. The camels walked all over her, herself and her brother. Grandfather did not count, because he could die at any moment.

She was sitting in the dwelling, just like any other day. They had just had their milk for breakfast. The little children had begun jumping around happily. The camel-herds had called to the camels one by one by their names. The camels had not answered until after one of the camel-herds had gone inside the camel-camp and hit them with his stick. He was a young boy, just as thin as her brother. The camels had come out. Early in the morning, her grandfather had told her to rise up and clean the milk vessels. It was the day that her grandfather had given her hand to the old man. Ebla had refused to go. She said that she was sick and suffering from stomach-ache.

'But go. Go and you will be all right,' said her grandfather.

'I cannot. I am sick.'

She felt disgusted. How could she get married to that man of all people. For once she hated her existence. Her grandfather had appealed to her, but Ebla would not hear of it.

'Then may you die,' he said.

The camel-herd had poked a camel in the ribs. The camel rushed out, jumping and kicking his legs in the air. The other camels followed suit. The camel-herds tried to stop them, but in vain. The camels went round and round at first and then ran towards the huts. Ebla was still lying on the floor, where her grandfather had left her when she refused to go and clean the milk-vessels. One of the camels ran into the hut, and walked all over her.

'Help me. Help me,' she shouted.

Nobody heard her.

She was on the brink of death, when two of the camel-herds came into the hut. Her grandfather was called in to give a final blessing, since everybody thought she would die, but he refused to.

Thank the Lord, all this was only a dream.

Ebla recovered from oblivion when she heard a familiar voice, enquiring if somebody by her name lived in the house. Ebla woke up from the dreadful sleep and day-dream, and jumped up to answer, 'Yes. I am here.'

It was the widow, and she had brought Ebla's brother along with her. Ebla felt subdued and betrayed as she met her brother. She did not know how to greet him or what words to say to him. 'They had just killed me,' her sub-conscious said to her. 'But it was not him. It was grand-father and the camel-herds.'

She and her brother stared at each other, then Ebla exchanged greetings with the widow before leading them to her room.

24

The sudden arrival of her brother

and the widow perturbed her. Why had they come? And why together? She had not asked her brother how her grandfather was – or, at least, how he had been when he left him. She hesitated for a while. 'Maybe I ought to ask him when we are alone,' she thought. 'Or he might have spoken to the widow – most probably he had.'

Till now, Awill's clothes were still with Asha, but the widow, making a remark just for the sake of making one, asked, 'Awill took every piece of his clothes with him?' Ebla wondered if she was just trying to find out something.

'No. No, he did not. I keep them elsewhere,' explained Ebla, not knowing that she had done wrong.

'Where?'

'In the landlady's room.'

'Why? There is enough space around. The room is practically empty,' said the widow.

'Awill did not have the money to buy me clothes. He was broke when he left,' said Ebla, changing the subject. Ebla's brother sat quietly on the bed. All he wanted to do was get back to the country quickly, he later told Ebla.

The widow did not notice the change of subject – one subject followed another. Ebla's brother remained quiet; he was always silent, as if he had made a resolution when he was in his mother's womb to speak only when spoken to. Ebla was worried about him.

'What about Grandfather – or don't you want to talk about him?' she asked as soon as the widow had left to take a bath.

'He is dead.'

'Grandfather. Dead? When?' she asked not really caring whether her grandfather lived or died.

'The day you left.'

'How?'

'He died.'

'Run over by a camel?'

'No.'

'Then how?'

'Of shock.'

'But why should he? I did not mean all that much to him, otherwise he would not have given my hand to that man.'

'What was wrong with that man?'

'With whom?'

'With the one Grandfather wanted you to marry?'

'I did not want to marry him.'

'Then what happened to you when you came to Belet Wene?'

'Our cousin did the same.'

'And then?'

Those 'and thens' were too much for her. She almost told him that Awill walked out on her, befriended a white girl in the white man's land and that she had done the same to him. She should not tell him. Or should she? Should she tell him everything, every scrap of it, every bit of it? Should she tell her brother that she had gone to bed with Tiffo, that she had married him last night and that he might come this evening to go to bed with her again – for she was his wife? Should she tell her brother every secret of hers? If she didn't, who else should she tell? Although he was very much younger, he was a boy, and therefore not as incapacitated as a woman. Although he was younger, he surely had better and more formidable and also more fascinating ideas. 'If his ideas are not very good ones, at least they are better than those of a woman like myself,' she thought.

'And then what happened?'

'What happened when?'

'After you came to Mogadiscio.'

'Nothing much,' Ebla answered.

Oddly enough, she persuaded herself not to be frightened of him any more. Why should she be? She knew that in the country a boy's word was higher than that of a girl, even if the girl was older. But that was not the case now. They were different. She thought that the situation was exactly the opposite of what it would have been if she had remained in the country.

'Why did you leave the beasts?' she asked.

'You also did, didn't you?'

'Because I am a woman.'

'And I am a man.'

'You don't have to remind me of that.' She thought, 'little whipper-snapper!'

'Neither have you any reason to remind me.'

'Are you going back now?' Ebla said to herself 'Out with it my boy!'

'Yes.'

'When?'

'As soon as you can send me back.'

'You don't fancy this place, is that the case?' she asked, hoping very much that it was.

'I loathe it. Half-naked women and crazy men, noisy places, men and women hand in hand, and all crazy people. They ought to be shot – all of them, even you.'

'Why?'

'Because they don't have any self-respect in them. You know, this place is full of people like yourself, all the outcasts, all those who could not get on well with their people in the country.'

'But it is good that they get on well together here.'

' "Birds fly with their own type of birds", the Somalis say. They are all of the same type here: misfits, filthy and mean.'

Ebla kept silent for a while. She thought it over, and she decided to send him back to the country as soon as he was ready to leave.

'Tomorrow morning,' he replied.

'I will send you back tomorrow morning.'

'*Ashantu*,' he said.

The widow came in. She had taken a lovely bath, she said, and asked them what they had decided.

'He is going back tomorrow,' said Ebla.

'Is he? I asked him to stay with you in Mogadiscio and join the schools here.'

'And they will make me a Gentile, eh?' he joined in. 'No! I don't want to be a black unbeliever.'

'Keep quiet. When older people talk, younger ones keep their mouths shut. Behave yourself. Be polite,' Ebla said angrily. She wished he had never come.

'So he won't hear of it?' the widow continued. 'I told him that he is lucky to have you. He could start primary classes,' (Ebla did not know this herself) 'and could become a teacher like Awill. You know Awill came to me when he was fourteen. That is the time he started going to school. And now he is a teacher, and he can speak Italian better than the white man. However, if your brother has decided to go back tomorrow, then I will take him back with me tomorrow. Only it will be very tiring for me to go tomorrow. I could do with a good rest.

'Tomorrow morning. I want to go tomorrow.'

In the evening they ate their dinner, and then slept. Asha lent them an extra bed and mattress. Ebla and her brother slept on one bed, adjacent to the entrance, away from the wall, where the widow was sleeping.

The widow read out the opening Sura of the Koran. That was her habit before she went to bed, she said, but Ebla could not remember that she had this habit when they were in Belet Wene. Anyway, Ebla fell asleep as soon as she lay on the bed.

Later there was a knock on the window; then a pause, then another knock; then a pause, then another knock, and a further pause.

The widow woke up. She thought it was an hallucination or some such feeling that one gets when one is in a new place.

'Ebla,' the widow heard a man's voice calling. Then the same thing happened all over again. This time Ebla awoke, and replied, 'Yes. What do you want? Who are you?'

'Tiffo,' he replied. 'I want to talk to you. Come to the window,' The widow pretended to be asleep, but as soon as Ebla joined Tiffo, she strained to hear what they were saying. She could vaguely hear, ' . . . My wife . . . she came . . . Asha. Tell her tomorrow morning . . . I am in trouble . . . will send a letter . . . as soon as possible.' Then they exchanged farewells and Tiffo left. The widow cancelled the notions she had formed the moment she heard the man calling to Ebla.

Back in bed, Ebla smiled to herself in the dark. 'Oh God in the heavens, it is great,' she thought. 'Tiffo will not come back to me. If what he says is true and he sends me the letter of divorce as soon as he can, then some of the problems will need no solution on my part. But if Awill comes home with the white woman, then I must do something about it to preserve my dignity. He can become a Gentile himself, but not at my expense.' In another few minutes, she fell asleep again.

The widow still wondered if her interpretation of the incident was correct. But she left for Belet Wene the following morning with Ebla's brother.

25

Ebla tried to make do with

whatever Tiffo gave her. But it required enormous patience to kill the anger and disappointments in him that she felt. He came to her place whenever he could, leaving behind some money, somewhere, underneath the pillow or on the table

He did this as he was leaving for his day's work, whatever it was. Ebla had become a sound sleeper of late, and she would never budge when he left.

Asha spoke to her about it several times. Ebla had no objection to Asha's unending, pretentious and unacceptable chatter. Today she would be annoyed with Tiffo and would put in a good word for Awill; tomorrow she would change her tune completely: 'Tiffo is the man you need,' she would urge Ebla. Only God knew what her reactions would be the third day, Ebla told herself. Beyond the shadow of a doubt, Asha was not pleased about the financial and marital behaviour of Tiffo.

'He treats you like a harlot,' she told her one day.

'How?'

'Well, that is the way they do it.'

'I don't understand.'

'Well, you are a fool, then. They give money to the harlots the way he gives it to you.'

'But I am not a harlot.'

'That is exactly what I say. You are not.'

'And I would not want to be one,' was Ebla's final word.

'Come what may, I am not going to act like a harlot. He is my husband.'

'But he doesn't associate as he does with his wife.'

Ebla thought over the question many a time, and finally she made up her mind. 'Asha doesn't have to tell me what to do and what not to do. I am twenty, or almost twenty. It is me who marries or is divorced, so she doesn't have to put her nose into my private business. I will tell her to keep out of it. In future, I am responsible for whatever I do. Tomorrow, I will tell her. Tomorrow. In future I will be myself and belong to myself, and my actions will belong to me. And I will, in turn, belong to them.'

Eventually she did manage to tell Asha to keep out of her own affairs. Then Ebla was happy, 'I am master of myself. The widow is not here. My cousin is not here. My brother has gone home and will never come back to give me orders. Tiffo is not here, so nobody can give me orders – at least, not until Awill comes home. And when he comes home, which will not be long now, I will tell him what he deserves. I am master of myself.'

Now Awill was expected any day. Ebla was uncertain about her stability. Tiffo had not stopped coming when his wife came to town, as she had expected. Instead, he came in the daytime, which made things worse for Ebla. Although she attempted to tell him what she thought about their 'secret marriage', which had nothing behind it except sharing a bed and earning some money from him, she hesitated. She just could not choose the right words to tell him, or even find time. One day – the day before Awill arrived back – Tiffo came to perform his task. They were in bed within a minute or two. The rituals of bed were over in no time.

'What a tiring day,' he said, after he had dressed.

'What did you do?'

'I left my wife and told her that I was going to do some business in town. I took my car and drove out, but then, the moment I reached the first bend, I could see her coming after me. Well, she did that several times, but I dodged her all the time. I stopped somewhere near the other bend where I guessed she would take a taxi. Then I stopped and waited. She came out, but could not find a taxi. So I parked my car at a place where she would not be able to notice. After that she returned home, biting her nails and she must have been swearing to herself,' he heaved up his belly and mumbled something irrelevant.

Ebla could not understand anything about cars. She had never been in one and she never wanted to ride in one. Whenever she went down to town, it was never beyond the market of Bondere and she always walked with Asha. Fortunately Asha was never prepared to pay a cent for a taxi. 'Why, better walk, and buy as many shoes as you can. And that won't cost you much. And why hurry? Start your journey early and naturally the bastards of shopkeepers will wait for you. If you cannot make it today, then wait till tomorrow.' That was what Asha had said, so why think about Tiffo's cars. Tiffo was silent. 'Frankness is the only resort,' thought Ebla.

'Does your wife know that you are married to another wife? Have you told her?' she asked him.

'No, she does not. And I have no intention of telling her. Why should she know?' he said, turning his face towards her, perhaps to have a better look now that she asked a question she had never dared to ask before.

'I know that you are married to another one, and I thought she might as well know about me.'

'She doesn't have to.'

'Supposing she does, what happens?'

'Nothing,' he said curtly.

'Tell her then.' She thought, 'you son of a bastard.'

'No.'

'Why?'

'Because I don't want to.'

'What is her name?' She wanted to add '. . . you spineless coward.'

'Why do you want to know?'

'You see, she is the other woman who shares you with me. Islam permits a man to marry four wives,' suggested Ebla, forcing a sly smile upon her face.

'I know.'

'Do you have two more except ourselves?' she wanted to add 'excluding whores that is.'

'Look, I am not going to be questioned by my wife, so don't speak to me like that.'

'No. No. Don't be angry. I just wanted to tell you one thing.' She said to herself, 'I must butter up the idiot.'

'Yes. Tell me.'

'I am also married.' She thought, 'how does that hit you?'

'To me. You are married to me. Ah! Ah!' he said, trying to be whimsical and witty as he could. He laughed a great belly-laugh, and then he checked himself.

'No. To another one. You see, you two take turns. When you used to come to me at night-time, his turn was day-time. You remember that night when you left for Baidoa in the morning and came in the evening, knocked on the window and told me about the arrival of your wife, do you remember that night?'

'Yes,' he said, and jumped up.

'He was here that night. And he was in bed with me. You remember I told you to go away immediately?'

'Yes. I remember that.'

'He was with me in bed. That was why I told you to go

away and leave me. I told you a lie, I told you I had just had my period.'

'What is his name?' he said. He gritted his teeth with anger.

'I will tell you only if you tell me the name of your wife,' said Ebla, blackmailing him.

'My wife's name is Ardo,' said he.

'Say "My other wife's name is Ardo", because I am also your wife. Don't forget that.'

'I won't forget that. But what is this man's name?'

'My other husband's name is Awill,' Ebla replied.

'You are telling me a lie.'

'No. I am not telling you a lie. Why should I? You have another wife and I have another husband. We are even: you are a man and I am a woman, so we are equal. You need me and I need you. We are equal.'

'We are not equal. You are a woman and you are inferior to me. And if you have another husband, you are a harlot,' said Tiffo, standing up, his lips and hands quivering. 'But I don't believe you.' He pointed his finger at her.

'Call Asha. Ask her if I am married to a man called Awill. Call her. It is a challenge.' She too was now bolt-upright.

Tiffo shouted to Asha, who came rushing and panting.

'Is this true?' asked Tiffo.

'Is what true?' asked Asha.

'That Ebla is the wife of Awill?'

After a little hesitation, Asha reluctantly said, 'Yes, she is.'

'Then you are divorced,' said Tiffo and walked away, pushing aside Asha, who stood in the doorway.

'Let me bring witnesses,' shouted Ebla after him.

'No need. I will keep my word. You are divorced,' he also shouted back.

Ebla did not care about the uproar this had created. 'Awill will come tomorrow. Tomorrow,' was all that she said. That night she had lovely dreams.

26

Ebla and Asha crouched on the ground, their hands resting on their laps, and their eyes fixed on the man whom they had come to consult. For no apparent reason, Ebla felt fatigued, and had it been possible to go away without hurting the feelings of others, and without causing any inconvenience to the man whose advice she had come to seek, she would have walked away. But the man was a *savant*, and he was going to make a prediction on which Ebla's life and destiny depended. Ebla did not feel uncomfortable inhaling the dust, but she felt it a bit choking. She got tired of making strokes and insignificant drawings on the ground. Her fingers were all dirty, her nails, long and uncut, looked very much out of shape, and her dress needed to be washed. She looked at it quickly and decided she would wash it as soon as she went home.

The man whom they came to consult did not possess the air of a *savant* and maybe that was what impressed Ebla most. Knowledge and blessings are bestowed by God upon those whom one never thinks highly of – that was what people said, and maybe it was true, Ebla thought. The man had a thick beard, untrimmed but combed nicely with the wooden comb which he had on his head: he looked like an Indian Sikh. He was not the type to swindle money out of people, Ebla assured herself. His belly protruded slightly forward and to a careless observer he might appear to be a rich man. He would caress his belly and mumble some inaudible words.

Ebla could not follow what he said, but Asha gave her frightening looks when she spoke. She therefore lost interest and sank into oblivion, which would not get her anywhere. There were many things to distract her attention, but she eventually decided, in spite of herself, that she must attend to the *savant*.

He counted the beads of his rosary, making it a point that Ebla and Asha would not count it with him, by hiding some under his thick hairy fingers. He counted the beads four times, and whenever he came to the red coral, which partitioned the black rosary beads into groups of thirty-three, he would stop to make a sign on the ground to represent what he had counted. The sign was either a dot or two dots. If the beads he counted were even, he would make two dots. And if odd, only one dot. When he marked one dot, he would use his forefinger, when two dots, any two fingers. Now that he came to the fourth round, Ebla and Asha sat patiently on the ground like cattle, waiting for the *savant* to speak out what he had seen.

The consultant seemed to be in distress. Wrinkles covered almost all his face, which was covered with scars. He frowned and licked his lips, perhaps as a sign of concentration.

'This fellow does not look happy about the outcome,' thought Ebla.

'What did you see?' enquired Asha. Ebla was unable to open her mouth. Although it was her problem, she was very young and it seemed most strange to her to talk to the man. But she had reluctantly agreed to let Asha deputize for her, make all the transactions and do all the talking connected with the issue.

'Something is obscure,' said the man.

'We have told you everything. Everything. We are not withholding any information,' Asha said.

'There is a gap somewhere,' said the man.

'Where?'

'In what you told me.'

Ebla decided to talk, but before she could, Asha motioned to her to keep out of the discussion.

'I cannot make predictions unless you tell me the whole story. There are many men in the life of this girl. Many. More than four. Actually the fourth is only represented by a streak of shadow – quite an insignificant matter.'

'We are not withholding anything from you,' Asha insisted, making an attempt to convince him.

He shook his head, indicating that he did not believe this. It was a great effort on Ebla's part to keep quiet. It was not her suggestion in the first place to consult this man. She had agreed to it because she thought she was in a miserable state of mind. Asha had convinced her of the truthfulness of the *Fal*, and Ebla succumbed again, but simply because there seemed to be nothing else to do.

'Tell me the whole story. Then I will tell you what I saw in the *Fal*.'

'We've told you everything.'

'I don't think so. You are wasting my time.'

'Is it a bad thing or is it a good thing that you saw in the *Fal*? Just tell us that, and we will pay your fee.'

'Not good and not bad.'

'Then what did you see?'

'She is sick. Somebody sent an evil-eye on her. It is very young and she can be cured.'

'By whom?'

'Don't take her to the hospital. Take her to a medicine-man, a priest and then he should read the Holy Book over her. Make it quick, otherwise something will happen to her, omething very awful.'

'When is the auspicious time?' Asha asked.

148

'Can you afford it today?'

Asha looked in the direction of Ebla who gave her approval by nodding her head.

'Yes,' Asha replied.

'Then do it today.'

'Here is your fee,' said Asha, handing him some money.

'Ten shillings? I don't accept it.'

'But you told us to pay you whatever we felt was suitable, so now I am paying you ten shillings.'

'It is not sufficient, it is very little. Add five, only five. I charge people according to their standard of living and I can guess that by looking at them.' Asha paid him another five as he asked and they left.

As soon as they entered the house, Ebla felt that there were lots of people there. She also saw one of the female tenants coming out of a room, carrying a small girl in her arms. The girl had her eyes closed, Ebla could see, and there were some blood spots on the dress of the woman who carried her. Ebla stood watching, and Asha went to her room, minding her own business. To her, perhaps, it was an everyday affair, as it was also to Ebla. But Ebla had supposed that the people in the towns had left that sort of thing. Now she could hear the drums being beaten and women talking at the tops of their voices.

'Oh, my God. What a painful thing it was,' she recalled. There were only two times that she wished she had not been born, and one of them was when she was circumcized. It was not only painful but a barbarous act, she thought. 'Are there people in the world who are not circumcised?' she wondered.

She recalled everything. They had sliced out her clitoris and stitched the lips together, thus blocking the passage-way, but also leaving a small inlet for urinating through. They had tied her legs together, and she had been lain flat on the ground without any mattress or anything underneath her, for she would bleed on it. They had beaten drums when the girls cried, so that the beating of the drums would drown the crying. If a girl cried too much, they tucked a piece of cloth into her mouth. The wound would not heal, they had said, if a boy saw it or a woman who had just committed adultery. So the girls had been confined in a hut for a period of between ten and twelve days.

She also recalled that other night of pain – the first time she had ever had sexual contact. It was with Awill, and it was very painful, indescribably painful. She had bled and he rejoiced seeing her blood, as his manhood depended upon breaking her chastity.

Now she stood motionless, watching. Asha came and spoke to her. Ebla did not hear, although Asha thought she had. Ebla went on thinking that because woman was created by God from the crooked rib of Adam, she is too crooked to be straightened. And anybody who tries risks breaking her. Maybe kidneys are called 'a woman's share of meat', because those men who eat kidneys are found to be of a lower, different category of men.

She straightened her dress, let her hands go over her chest, and went towards her room.

It dawned upon her that she could call upon Asha, which she did. The latter told her that she had sent for a Sheikh, and, as soon as he came, she would call her.

27

Back in her room as she lay on
her bed, Ebla meditated at length, opening and closing her
eyes as the wind blew upon them.

Asha had told her that the Sheikh who would read the
Koran over her had been sent for. She thought to herself,
'What is life? There is no difference between town and
country, or between Tuesday, Wednesday, Thursday,
Friday, Saturday, Sunday, Monday, Tuesday: back to where
it began. There is no beginning of this world and no end
either. It moves on and on, in a circle, or along itself, or
round itself, or abreast itself. This world is routine, life is
routine. People don't get surprised (as one might expect)
when their beloved sons, daughters or friends disappear into
the ground. God has taken them away. They don't get
affected or moved when a new-born baby comes into the
world to create disturbance. Instead, they cut the throats of
other animals to rejoice on the occasion. What is the use of
life? Especially for a person like myself? I am nothing but
an object. I am nothing. I did not cost Awill anything: he
did not pay me or any relation of mine any dowry. He did
not even know who my relations were in case I wanted him
to pay my dowry to someone else. Maybe it is because I did
not cost him anything that Awill started running after
another woman, a white woman, who doesn't believe in
God, a Gentile, a white woman.

'I wonder if it is true that God has said that "a woman's
prophet and second-to-God is her husband". If this is true,

then life is not worth living. Why, Awill runs after another woman (a white woman, worst of all) and then when he has done whatever he wanted with her, he comes back to me and I have to wash his legs, cook his food and seek no other shelter but his abode, and I can consider it mine too only if he wants me.

'I cannot recall when I came here. Neither can I look back without feeling disgusted. Usually I am so confused, but each time that it seems to be improving, something happens which leaves me in the same old situation. Am I cursed? And if so who has done it?'

Ebla felt that her ribs ached. So she turned over on to her other side. She kept on thinking, rationalising all that had happened to her.

'I am guilty of one thing: my marriage to Tiffo. I should perhaps have waited for a while, but I was bitterly annoyed and I wanted to take revenge upon Awill. But what did that do to me? Whom did it benefit – him or myself? In any case, I was the victim. I went to bed with a man, and although I was doing it deliberately, I could see the consequence. I never met the man to whom my cousin gave my hand, neither did I care for the other fellow, whatever his name was. They were not my husbands, and so they could never be prophets to me. You only obey the orders of prophets when you have embraced their doctrines. But I am a woman, and for a woman there are many limitations. For one thing, Awill could marry another woman and bring her home, and I would not be able to say a word. He could marry three more, if he wanted to. I wish he would do that. Maybe dwelling in hell is preferable to being its neighbour – as long as the heat is no greater. I wonder if I am a prostitute; I wonder how many people think that I am one.'

She recalled an incident in the country in which a woman who was selling her body had been found out. Her relatives seized the man who was in bed with her, and beat him until every part of his flesh ached. Then they got hold of the woman and burnt her house and all her possessions. She had been stigmatized until one day she left the country and came to Mogadiscio, and took up prostitution as her profession. What good had her relatives done? A person is tempted to do awful things once in a while, but violence doesn't solve any problem; violence and harsh beating alone could never have made that woman repent for her sin. But was it sin? 'What is sin? If only I knew.

'I love life. I love it. Everybody loves it, each in his own way. Even death is nothing but the other side of life, and anyone who loves to die naturally loves to live. I love to live for something, but I don't mind dying for the same thing. I love life. I love all its colours. I love nature. I love rain. I love spring. I love misery and hunger. But I do not love these things because they bring about either happiness or sadness: for me here there is no longer happiness or sadness. I love animals, which are the only part of nature that I know. That is my fate – to be able to communicate with these things which I know.

'I have never done anybody any harm and I have no such intentions. I have never told lies, and I've never uprooted generations of people, but who is responsible for my miserable situation? God or myself? Naturally if things turn bad, we always put the blame on someone else, so what is better than putting all the censure on God? But honestly who is responsible? Partly Awill. Why? Because he left me in the lurch. But surely he was sent out of the country to do something, wasn't he? Then perhaps it is my family who are responsible. But how? Because they never brought me into contact with suitable men? But who is "my family" anyway? My grandfather had died even before my brother came here, and my father's and mother's bones had been reduced to dust a long time back. But the other relations, do I have any? I wonder if I do. My inexperience of life was partly responsible. I would probably have made a clean breast of everything and then forgotten about it if I had known what I was doing. It is because of human weakness that one prefers the unattained or the undone or the unknown to what has happened in the past. Well, that is for each person to think out for himself. Now my problem concerns my men, and it is a great pity that they are not in the least bit worried about the situation. I am turning over in this bed, thinking out solutions to these problems. They may be sleeping with other women for all I know – they could be doing anything.

'Divorce. Should I ask for a divorce? Our religion is very strict towards women in this respect. The concessions given to men are far too great: it seems that religion is the only right thing. Oh, my God, I don't actually mean this. You hear me, God; I repent. I repent to Thee. Nothing is wrong with our religion.

'But will I or won't I ask for a divorce? How can I ask Awill to divorce me? I will feel lonely, and isolated. My soul has never had a partner and it will never get one, not even in the next world, because I have committed so many errors as it is. I have committed adultery: I have broken God's law, but God is quite merciful, though when He punishes, He can be cruel. One never knows whether one will be treated with mercy or punished, though.

'I never understand myself,' Ebla continued thinking. 'I just never do. The prophets say that everybody's fate is written on God's slate. Everything is recorded up there – or is the record made down here? Are there angels who rest on your shoulders and record your doings? On the face of the moon, there is a big tree, and each leaf on that tree represents an individual. One dies when one's leaf falls off the tree on the moon. The leaf withers when a person has been in bed for a long time. But I respect God and He knows that I do, and I promise that I will say my prayers five times a day as usual if my wish is fulfilled.

'But what do you want? I wish I knew. I am a woman now, a grown-up girl; I am a woman, and because I am in trouble, my womanhood is evident. Men have woman-troubles, but it doesn't upset them as much as it does us. I am a woman, and because my blood-money is half that of a man, it is apparent that I am an inferior being to him. We cannot say that God has done something wrong. He, the Almighty God, is the one who has fixed the status of human beings. He made me cost half of a man, and He must have had a good reason for doing so, otherwise why did He do this to me? I am a woman, and because I am tempted more than a man, my weakness comes to light faster than it would in the case of a man. I look at a man and I am tempted: if I yield to this temptation, the consequences are so bitter that the taste of it may result in my losing my own existence.

'Oh, my God, if only men knew how women are tempted! We may say no, give a flat refusal, but inwardly we desire the man more than he desires us. Arrawello, the wisest Somali female who ever lived, gave her fellow-women some advice before she died. She said, "Ye women, say 'No' even if afterwards you come to regret it. Be obstinate, and let no man shake your feminine resolve. And be respectful and also decent." I wonder if she wasn't wiser than the men who were apparently superior to her.

'But why didn't I say "No" to Awill? I wonder if he would have insisted on marrying me? But I would have eventually said "yes" anyway.

'If I had not left the country and instead had married the old man my grandfather had given my hand to, maybe I would not have run into all these troubles,' Ebla thought. 'I have never regretted doing anything in my life. Why should I? I am weak in the sense that I accept whatever an older person dictates to me. But I don't mean to harm anybody: I want to make the best of what I have, but at the moment this is everlasting troubles and headaches. My belly turns over whenever I regret. It is not good. It doesn't help matters. Whatever I do is something in my nature, which I cannot help. The only way, maybe, is to take a knife and cut my throat, but I am a woman and I cannot do that – I lack the courage.

'I look as dejected as a camel which has lost its only calf. My only advantage over a camel is that I can try to reason with myself, and speak out. But to whom can I speak? Maybe only to God, to whom I have not addressed any prayers for such a long time that I cannot remember the last time. One by one I am losing my acquaintances, and even my relations. I have lost my only brother's confidence: he will never come and see me again. It is the same with my cousin and his wife: they would bake me alive. Asha has no more use for my friendship, and I don't know anybody else in this place. There is no friendship between a husband and a wife; the husband is a man and the wife is a woman, and naturally they are not equal in status. Friends should be equal before they can become friends. If you despise or look down upon somebody, he cannot be your friend, neither can you be his friend.

'First thing in the morning, I will buy myself guavas,' she decided. 'The prophet has said that if you eat guavas and die within forty days, your entrance to heaven is guaranteed. I will ask Asha to buy me some, but she must not know the reason why I want them, for she would envy my entrance to heaven and would buy me something else. I wonder what a guava tastes like: it must be bitter, I suppose, or perhaps sour. Despite its taste, I am going to eat it. Do they grow guavas here near the sea? What does the sea look like? Huge blue water they've told me. Guavas are probably blue also like the sea. And do they taste like salt? Sea water is salty, Asha said, and anything which grows in the coastal area must be salty. Far away in the country, we suffer because of lack of water, but in the towns they have plenty of it – rivers, seas and lakes. Our beasts in the country die of thirst, but here they don't have as many beasts as we have, and yet they have this huge surplus of water. That is life: when you need something you don't get it, and when you don't need it, there is plenty. I wonder if it is ever possible to have as many things as one wants.'

Someone whistled a tune Ebla was not familiar with. The sound came from outside although she thought for a second that it was from within the room. Ebla wished she could go and tell the person to stop whistling because at the sound of whistling the genies come in the night, and either the whistler gets whacked in the face or this happens to those around him who should have told him not to whistle. Why should a person whistle? But then again why shouldn't he?

Ebla came out to speak to the person concerned, but just as she reached the doorway, and as she was leaning against the wall, feeling a little weak and unbalanced, she saw a meteor falling. In spite of herself, she could not help shouting, 'Fall. Fall. Fall on those who don't believe in God the almighty. Fall on them.'

Then she bit her little finger. She looked around and saw dark figures squatting outside the other rooms. She felt disappointed that they did not wish the same thing. 'Maybe they don't hate those who do not believe in God in the way that I do,' she thought.

Then she went inside. The whistling had stopped. Ebla stretched herself on the bed again and continued her speculation.

'I am a naturally confused person, but though the Creator is responsible for his creation, I am responsible for my actions. Let me analyse my men: I wonder if I should consider in this case the first one, from whom I escaped. It was because of him that I ran away, and it is really on account of him that everything else has happened to me. God sees all that happens and He knows everything in my mind. Giumaleh was not known to me in the first place. I never saw him, and nor did the Sheikh pronounce our engagement. It was only verbally done between him and my grandfather. Dirir is in the same boat: he was not known to me personally and I never set eyes on him. He simply made an arrangement with my cousin.

'But Awill – he was the only husband I married willingly. Maybe I would not have married him if I had not been running away. I would have thought it over. But he took advantage of my situation and an elopement was all right with him. In the beginning, he was rude to me, but in the end, he changed his attitude. We only spent ten days together, but now his affair with that woman in the photo has naturally broken the mirror of my heart. It has split my heart into smaller pieces, and it is impossible for my heart ever to be the same again. Oh, if only he knew this – perhaps he would leave me or perhaps he would come closer to me, do the unexpected and lie near me, and be friends with me again. But supposing he learns about Tiffo? Just suppose he does, what will happen?

'About Tiffo, there is not much to say. He is a man of money, the richest man I have met in my life. But I have not met many, have I? Maybe if I were after money and riches, I could stay back in the country and marry the man to whom my grandfather had given my hand for marriage: he was as old as Tiffo and probably as fat.

'I am responsible for the death of my grandfather,' she thought. This was the end of her talk to herself.

'With tomorrow's sun maybe happiness will come to me,' she said aloud. And then she slept without eating her supper.

28

Ebla woke up the next morning more pre-occupied than ever. She had had a bad dream the night before. The morning sun was bright, and she imagined that nature had become bolder, exposing its brilliance and brightness like this in its simplest form. She thought that she had walked out on nature and that now it would give her slaps across the face, stab her from behind with a poisonous dagger or make her lag behind the children of nature. Nature would always make her lag behind others, she felt. She thought to herself that one lived a parody of existence if one did not get the essential and basic satisfaction of life. Life was like a dress (what an analogy!) and one's change of status was like a change of dress. It would be monotonous to have the same dress on for ever. 'Life is simpler than we think,' she decided, smiling peevishly into the face of life, which was represented by the room she was in. 'It is only we who don't understand life, or rather we tend to misunderstand it,' she said aloud.

With her hand she felt down her body, naked under the sheet; she scratched her sex, then chuckled. 'This is my treasure, my only treasure, my bank, my money, my existence.' She let her hand lie upon it for a while, and wondered if she had not got tired of playing uninteresting games with foolish men on beds. The area of her sex was slightly damp. Then she let her hand go up towards the belly: it was soft and uneven. Then she touched her navel and picked out some dirt. She looked at the dirt hanging on her nails, then threw it under the bed. She covered herself from the tip of her toes to the top of her head with the sheet. She looked into herself and found something new about herself. She looked into herself literally – a thing which she had never done before. She had never bothered about her bodily make-up, thinking that this was more the business of the man who was interested in her. Now she realized that the changes she had undergone were amazing. Stretching her legs and raising her head a little bit, she discovered that she was getting older. Her flesh was soft and fluffy, and she looked like a woman of thirty. Her lips had cracks, as though they had been kissed by unknown devils. Her tongue had broken reddish spots in the middle under the palate. Her breasts were as soft as butter: they hung from her chest, not forming an integrated part of her body, as if they had never been a part of her at all. She thought she had lost the game: she had become a prostitute without realizing that she had become one. She then uncovered her body down to the belly. She did not re-position her head, and thus could not see anything beyond the two hills of her breasts. She touched her left breast, and, as if she thought that the other one would get jealous of being over-looked or something, she hurried to give it a touch, a cajoling touch, patting it on the nipple. She squeezed both of them like you squeeze a lemon with no juice in it. The corns inside the breasts were smaller in size. She pressed hard and it hurt. She closed her eyes, wandering into nothingness and creating in her mind something which had never existed before, and which would never exist.

Suddenly there was a knock on the door, followed by a pause.

'Open the door,' said a woman's voice and Ebla knew that it was Asha. 'Open the door and come out. The Sheikhs have come. Hurry up. Wake up.' Ebla made her voice sound as if she had just woken up and said that she would come out very soon.

Just in front of Asha's room, two men sat cross-legged on the straw mat laid on the ground. They both had white robes on and Ebla could see that they were anxious to get through with the whole thing quickly. From inside her room, she could notice their movements.

The morning was young, and Ebla felt empty inside. Her brain was hollow and she knew that she would walk tensely. It was an effort on her part to walk the hundred paces that divided them, for her legs were tired and her head was exceptionally heavy, as the daylight shone upon her. Ebla pulled herself together and came towards the Sheikhs who were silent – determined; but only God knew what about.

The elder of the two Sheikhs beckoned to her to take the seat to their left and wished her '*Nabad*' – maybe on behalf of his partner as well, as he looked in his direction immediately after uttering the greeting. Ebla mumbled back hers, fixing her gaze upon Asha.

The elder one said, 'How are you this morning?' sounding as if he had seen her yesterday.

'Better,' replied Ebla.

'I hope you will feel much better in another five minutes or so, after I have been through with you.'

He lifted a wooden slate he had brought with him, glancing first at his friend, whom he was perhaps consulting, and then at Ebla, perhaps to see her reaction. The younger Sheikh silently handed him the ink-pot, and the elder one carried it away, gripping it from the bottom, and placed it on the middle of his palm. He then asked Ebla if she knew where they could get a razor blade.

'What for?' she said in a frightened voice, for she thought they were going to operate on her.

'Not to cut you with,' the Sheikh said humorously, 'But for some other purpose.'

'As it is, I have enough cuts on my body,' Ebla continued, forgetting that the Sheikh had said that he would not cut her with it. She remembered yesterday's barbarous operation of circumcision and the day they operated upon her; she remembered also the day she lost her virginity, the pain she underwent, and how she had bled under Awill's manhandling.

Before Ebla could stand up, Asha reappeared on the scene.

'Wait. Don't go. Asha will get us one,' said the Sheikh, and told her what to bring him.

'Yes. I will get it.'

Asha soon returned with the blade, then the elder Sheikh started sharpening the yellow reed with it. He hummed a religious song to himself as he cut the edge. The waste showered upon the straw-mat. He lifted the wooden slate, dipping the reed pen in the ink-pot, and wrote some Arabic inscriptions, which Ebla supposed to be the Koran. He filled the slate, then he spoke to Asha again and asked for a glass of water and an empty vessel.

Asha brought the glass, then the Sheikh raised the slate, its sharp end resting on the mouth of the vessel, and he poured the water down from the top of the slate and washed the ink blottings into the vessel. When he had done this, he stopped for a while and said, 'May the Lord bless us, Amen.'

'Amen,' mumbled Asha and the other Sheikh.

'Amen,' repeated Ebla after them.

'Now then, drink this,' said the Sheikh.

With thanks Ebla accepted the vessel, full of the polluted water, darkened with ink which was made out of coal and glue.

She emptied the glass in no time. 'Good,' said the Sheikh. 'You will be all right from now on,' he assured her. 'Any time there is any trouble, do come and tell me. Asha knows the family whom I stay with. Now I will go,' he announced.

'No. No. Stay for lunch.'

'I can't. I must go and deliver my lecture to my students. They will be waiting for me in the mosque.'

'Excuse us for bothering you,' Asha said.

The Sheikhs got up and walked away, Asha accompanying them to the gate. Ebla remained seated and looked in their direction: she could see Asha touching the Sheikh by the shoulder, then she unclasped her palm, thus giving him some money, but Ebla did not know how much.

Asha came back and told Ebla to go and take a rest. 'I will wake you up for lunch,' Asha added.

'How much did you pay him?'

'Not much. Don't worry. Go to sleep. It will help you.'

Once she was in bed again, Ebla felt like vomiting and her stomach turned over in such a way that she felt dizzy. She felt nauseated, groaned and closed her eyes. Because she felt hot also, she got out of bed to close the door and undo her dress. Her breasts were full, and she felt strange as she touched them. She let her hand go over them, and, as she did so, she saw the skin around the nipples looked darker in colour. She imagined that she was pregnant.

'But whose baby is it? Not Tiffo's, oh my God!'

Suddenly she wanted to urinate, but, finding that the only toilet in the building was engaged, she walked over to Asha's room. Asha met her on the way.

'What happened? I thought you were in bed. Why didn't you go and take a rest?'

'I am waiting for the toilet.'

'Stomach trouble?'

'No. Only urine, but do you have lemons?'

'No. But I can get them for you.'

'Don't bother,' said Ebla.

'You feel something?'

'No.'

'Are you sure?'

'Yes,' replied Ebla.

'Not pregnancy or something?'

'No. Not that I know.'

'The toilet is free now. Go, run before it is occupied by somebody else.'

Ebla obeyed and ran into the toilet. She came out pale and panicky. Asha had gone down town by then. Ebla picked up a piece of coal and brushed her teeth with it, like a tooth-brush. She swallowed some liquefied coal unintentionally, and felt quite herself again. She then picked up a square piece of clay and chewed at it. All these were signs of preg-nancy and she knew this perfectly well.

But she just wanted to know whose baby it was she had in her womb. Whose? 'Awill will come home very shortly. Tiffo might come and claim me as his wife any time. I am a man's property for sale.'

Ebla pulled herself together and walked to her room. She took the mirror, held it in front of her and looked into it. She saw someone who did not look like herself, someone who had become pale and had a blank face, with many contours and round cheeks. It was someone unlike herself. She chuckled at her image. 'Thank goodness we don't look like our images,' she comforted herself. 'And if I did, would anyone look at me, let alone marry me?

'A man or a woman – who cheats who?' she asked herself. 'Maybe I should put these questions to other people. And, since this image is not myself, why don't I use it? I will do the talking.

'Man?' she spoke in a female voice.

'Yes,' she replied with a masculine voice.

'Do you cheat women?'

'No.'

'Do they cheat you?'

'Yes.'

'What must you do about them?'

'Cheat them.'

• 'Who is more important, you or a woman?'

'There are no two opinions about that.'

'How?'

'I am the one who is active in bringing about anything, in bed and out of bed.'

'Do you think you could live happily without women in the world?'

'Yes, quite happily.'

'The interview with you is over,' she said in a whisper.

Then she laughed into the mirror. Man not a cheat? A will not a cheat? Tiffo not a cheat? A woman is unimportant?

She laughed into the mirror again, slobbering upon it, smudging the surface with saliva. Cleaning it with her robe, she could vaguely see the figure behind it. 'Woman?' she asked in a grunting male voice, 'Are you a cheat?'

'Sometimes.'

'But why?'

'Because men cheat me.'

'But why?'

'I take my revenge upon them.'

'Yes, but why?'

'I don't know. I am innocent. I don't know what to do. I just don't know what I do sometimes. I do things, just do them without really getting myself involved. I put my faith in my man, but once I lose it, then it is hard to regain it. It is jealousy and insecurity that causes most misunderstandings. What do you men do about these things?'

'Continue doing things secretly until I am discovered or caught red-handed. What would you do?'

'Appeal to them. They are beasts and are stronger than we are. Therefore we must cut the ground from under them and cheat by appealing to them, smile at them and speak nicely to them.'

By moving the mirror a little bit to the left, she saw Asha's image. She threw the mirror down and silently stared at Asha, with hungry eyes.

Without saying anything, Asha walked away.

29

It was about lunch-time. Ebla

was in bed half asleep and half awake, half hungry and half thirsty, but unwilling to stir out of bed. She felt sour in the tongue and bitter in the belly – a sign of pregnancy, she reminded herself. But there was no reason to get shirty about it, for this was a woman's role, and one has to play one's role. 'Why should I grumble if I am giving life to another person – a baby, my own baby? Why? There can be no good harvest without hard labour, thus bodily torture is my hard labour. This bodily torture is what I inherited from my mother. She was a woman too.'

Ebla remembered one day when she was still in the country. She went down to the next hut in the dwelling, to get some wood for her fire. She and the daughter of the family started talking. While they were talking, the younger brother and sister of that girl rushed in and asked where their mother was.

'What is it you want from mother?' their elder sister had asked them.

'The Idd festival is approaching. I want my mother to buy me some clothes,' said the boy.

'You see, sister, this is a boy and he doesn't want to listen. I told him that I am a girl and he is a boy. Girls should ask their mothers, boys their fathers. So tell him to go and talk to father.' After making a great deal of noise, it was agreed that they should wait for their parents. It was this incident involving these children who were no more than infants, that had reminded Ebla of her sex. Until now, it had not dawned upon her that what the children had said had any sense in it.

Ebla now sat up in bed, waiting for a call from Asha to say that lunch had been prepared. 'What would I do without Asha?' thought Elba. 'I scold her when I want things, I call her names, but without her, I would now be a forsaken woman. Maybe I would even end up by becoming a prostitute. I don't know how to thank her, I just don't know how. Maybe she understands that I am grateful; I hope that she understands, for without her, I would be doomed.'

Instead of shouting to Ebla, Asha came to her.

'How are you?' she asked Ebla.

'Fine.'

'Still feeling something in the stomach?'

'Yes. But relatively small.'

'Have you missed the flow?'

Ebla jerked her head. 'I don't know,' she added.

'Well come. We shall have lunch.'

But before she was fully dressed Tiffo suddenly appeared at the door. Asha was bending down to tighten her shoes and did not see him until he came in.

'What do you want?' said Ebla, pulling her dress to cover her naked thighs and ribs.

'Nothing,' said Tiffo and grinned.

'Then why did you come?' blurted out Asha. 'If you don't want anything why did you come?'

'Can't I come when I feel like it?'

'Yes,' said Asha.

'No,' said Ebla.

Then Ebla and Tiffo looked at each other, both smiling sheepishly.

'Well, then I came because I wanted to come. That is all.'

'We were just going to have lunch,' Asha said.

'Is that an invitation to join you?'

'No,' said Asha. 'You fool. No invitations for you.'

'You know I came to talk to Ebla, not to you,' Tiffo said. 'So why don't you keep out of it?'

'She is not going to keep out of it,' said Ebla. 'She is responsible for me here.'

'She is your advocate, is she?' asked Tiffo, half in Somali and half in Italian. Ebla looked blank, for she did not understand what 'advocate' meant.

'I am her advocate,' said Asha.

'Is she?' asked Tiffo, looking towards Ebla. Ebla gave him a glance and then looked in Asha's direction.

'Yes,' she said in a low voice, 'But do you mind going out while I dress. I will call when I am ready.'

'Well, then maybe I should get myself an advocate.'

'Didn't you divorce Ebla?' asked Asha, as soon as they stood outside.

'Yes.'

'Then what do you want?'

'I just want to get something straightened out before events get beyond our control and before we start regretting the day we were born. I am sure that biting one's lip doesn't solve any problem.'

'Now we can go back, Ebla is dressed,' said Asha. 'But what do you want to straighten out?' she went on, as they re-entered the room.

'Maybe I should think it over and come back when I have reached a conclusion or some sort of understanding with myself.'

'But what is it that you want to straighten out?' repeated Asha, giving him a sheepish and altogether unexpected smile. 'We can help you get things straightened out.'

'You see, my wife has heard about my marriage to Ebla. As soon as she came to Mogadiscio yesterday, she started looking for Ebla. She came to me only after she had been unable to locate her. My wife is a vicious woman and said that she will kill Ebla when she meets her.'

'Why? Why should she even want to kill her? It is awful that she said such a thing, but does she think that she can get away with it? They will cut her into pieces. But why does she want to do it?' said Asha.

'Because Ebla married me. That is why she wants to kill her.'

'But that is not Ebla's fault,' retorted Asha.

'Neither is it mine. And I know that it is not my wife's at all. But she and her relations have done this killing many many times and they have never been caught – they have always got away with it. I don't know how they do it, but they bribe the police officers and the judges. I realize that it is unjust to do that to Ebla, since it was I who married her. She was only a partner – not a party to it. I hope you see that difference,' said Tiffo.

'Have you told your wife that you divorced Ebla a long time ago?' Asha questioned him.

'Yes. I have told her, but she doesn't seem to believe it.'

'Then what does she want?'

'She said she wants to see the woman who shared me with her. Just to see her, she said. But I know that she will do some other thing.'

'Like what?'

'Beat her up.'

'But she cannot beat her in our presence, can she?'

'Yes,' said a voice from behind Asha.

Ebla saw four women standing side by side, all ungaitered and ready to fight. The one who had spoken was hefty, dark and impressive. When she smiled a gold tooth showed in her lower front teeth. Ebla was terrified. She then looked at the others, who all looked alike, short, dark and handsome. Probably because of the tension she didn't notice Asha.

'What do you want, Ardo?' appealed Tiffo to the one who spoke, who was his wife.

'I said I wanted to see the woman, didn't I?' she lashed back at him.

'Yes.'

'Then let me see.'

'But now that you've seen her, why don't you go away?'

'I am not ready to go away,' she said sneeringly through her teeth.

Ebla stood up, prepared herself for a fight, tightening her dress round her belly. She did this, thinking that nobody was watching her. But one of the women had seen her, and whispered something into Ardo's ears. Ebla guessed what it was. 'So what' she thought.

'But go back to your house, Ardo,' said Tiffo appealingly. 'Please go,' he said.

'If you don't stand aside, I am going to beat you with this shoe,' said Ardo, taking off a shoe and moving towards him.

Tiffo shrank back, like a rat which had just seen a cat. He touched his belly and adjusted his belt, then said:

'But go now.'

Ebla thought, 'What a husband! Supposing all women were like her, what a world this would be?'

'No. I won't.'

'I will call the police.'

Ebla sneered inwardly, 'Better call all your kith and kin as well!'

'Call the police and have me arrested. You will have to bring me food when I am in prison, but now, if you don't keep quiet, I will beat you with this shoe.'

This time she moved forward, stretched her arm and was about to hit him, when Asha said, 'No, don't do that in our presence. You look between your legs, and be careful.'

Ardo looked, and when she saw Asha stopped.

'Asha, are you here? I only meant to beat him and then come and tell you afterwards. Did you know that he was the husband of this woman?' she said pointing her finger at Ebla contemptuously.

'But he no longer is. Now that I have told you, will you go out of my house? We know each other. You remember everything, our fights and friendships. I don't want you coming in to use my house; if you want to beat your husband go and do it outside my house. But Ebla is under my responsibility, and you can't touch her with your little finger. Let us be peaceful with each other.'

'I will go. I will go quickly,' Ardo said, as she threw her shoe on the floor, put it on and beckoned to the others to follow her.

'You and I will settle our dispute when you come home,' she said to Tiffo. The female invaders left, and so did Tiffo, leaving Ebla and Asha alone.

'Did you know Ardo before?'

'Yes. We knew each other in Baidoa. We grew up together. We had lots of fights. She doesn't look as old as I do, does she?'

'No,' replied Ebla.

'She is older than I, but I beat her many times when we were still young and unmarried. She knows she cannot afford to have troubles with me. Those women always go together and beat their four husbands together. It is a crime doing that.'

'Are all of them married?'

'Yes – only officially married. But you see they marry and divorce their men when they like, just the way they want.'

'But that is contrary to our religion.'

'They don't care about religion, they are such crooks. Poor fellows, their husbands. One of them is an extremely nice fellow. I have known him since childhood. He is married to the youngest. They beat him when they don't want him to talk about his unhappy marriage. They beat him inside the bars, on the main streets and in his house. He has had a tough time. I met him the other day and I told him to divorce her (or them, for they are always together) and I would protect him from being beaten. But they are not too bad, otherwise, it is just their men-troubles and men really ought to be beaten.'

'Sometimes,' said Ebla.

'I am going down town in another hour or two. Do you want to come with me?'

'Yes. I want to come.'

But before they left for town, Asha and Ebla transferred Awill's belongings back to the room, and re-arranged it exactly as it had been when he left for Italy.

30

Ebla and Asha went down town
to shop. Ebla had not been to many places in Mogadiscio, and
every time that she saw something new to her, she would say
to herself repeatedly, 'This is not my place. I am an intruder.
Inwardly I feel like my brother, although my nature is
different and my emotional make-up is cooler than his.' But
she would brush aside such objections which kept forcing
themselves into her mind.

While they were still out shopping, Awill arrived back at
the house. Somebody told him where Ebla was likely to have
left the key in case she was out. Opening the room, he found
that almost everything was as he had left it. There was
nothing more, nor less. Awill walked around searching for
something, but he did not know what. Then suddenly he
saw beneath a plate leaning against the window-pane the
photo of that Italian girl which he had sent to Jama a long
time ago. He could hardly believe his eyes at first.

'How can it be?' he said aloud, as if speaking to someone
else. 'Jama, the bastard. He gave me away. I knew he would.
It is the region where he comes from. There nobody confides
in anybody. Why did he bring her the photo? I did something wrong, but is it such a big crime – and against whom
is it a crime? I like Ebla. I did not like her at first when we
were married – how could I? I hardly knew her, but I like
her more now and I don't want to lose her because of girls
who were just a pastime. You go and visit a country. You
befriend a girl from that country, and then you talk about it

to friends afterwards. But I never intended to marry her or take her seriously. She was just there to help kill the time.'

Turning around, Awill found Ebla standing in the doorway. He kept quite still.

'I have been listening,' said Ebla.

'Who told you that I had come back?'

'The woman who directed you to where the key was. She told me that you had come.'

'*Nabad*,' he said.

'*Nabad*,' she replied, forcing a smile on her face. She didn't move.

'You've grown fatter,' he said, his hands in his pockets, watching her curiously.

'Have I?' she said, 'And you've got thinner.'

'Have I lost weight?' he asked.

'Yes. Maybe because you ate pork.'

He kept quiet.

'Tell me, did you?'

'We've just met. Let us talk about something else, shall we?'

'Yes. But what? What is wrong in asking if you ate pork?' said she, coming into the room now and throwing her shawl on the bed.

'Who told you that I ate pork? It is funny. I mean what we are talking about. We have not even exchanged greetings yet.'

'Yes, we have. The necessary greeting is over,' she said.

'Oh, yes. Well, yes, I did eat pork, and it is delicious.'

'That is what makes you look thinner. You ate something forbidden by our religion. It is a bastard's diet. It does not agree with your stomach and you will get sick – worms and all that.'

'I only ate it twice,' Awill said.

'And did you drink?'

'Look, let us stop talking like this. I am tired. I want to take a bath and have a little nap and then talk. Didn't my aunt come here?'

'Yes. How did you know?'

'She wrote to me.'

'She brought my brother along with her, but he did not like Mogadiscio. You know my grandfather has died.'

'Did you have a grandfather?'

'Yes. I had one and I told you about him. You have a very bad memory: one day you will forget that I am your wife.'

'No, I won't. I won't.'

Inwardly she felt an urge to get down to brass tacks, to stop this sort of talk and finalize all her doubts. However, she was so tired of all these escapades, which didn't benefit her in the least. Maybe problems would solve themselves, she thought.

'Did Jama give you any money?'

'Yes,' Ebla said.

She was in a state of suspense. She looked at his dark, handsome, well-framed face and wondered if she could guess what he was thinking about. His profile showed a long nose, and the chin was sharper than she had thought. Ebla started as if to say something to him, but nothing came out. She just stared at her husband, who had just come back from the land of the foreigner, and she was uneasy. His silence made her uneasy. Even if she wanted to talk, what could she say to him?

'Why didn't you ask your brother to stay?' Awill asked.

'I asked him to, but he refused.'

'Why didn't you insist?'

'Why should I? If he didn't want to, then it was best that he should go back to the country.'

'What will he do in the country?'

'Look after the beasts, of course. What else would he do? Count how many stars there are in the sky during daytime. Those beasts are our wealth, they are all that we possess in this world, he and I. I am here, a wife, and he ought to be there – and it was a mistake in the first place for him to have come here.'

'But he will die ignorant. He will not have learnt anything before the earth eats away his bones. That will be the first lesson of life for him.'

'People here in Mogadiscio and in towns don't have the slightest idea how to take care of beasts, how to milk them, how to love them, how to sacrifice their own lives to make the beasts happy and fat and healthy. They know how to eat meat and drink milk, but that is all they know. How ignorant and proud they are! A white man's language is no knowledge.'

'But loving the beasts was what you ran away from, wasn't it? Don't forget you own self. I wonder if women will ever decide what they want. Why are you all so undecided; why are you all so insecure?'

'Because we don't have anywhere else to run to. Our only refuge lies in indecision and we don't know if our decisions will bear fruit.'

'It is a mistake on your part to have sent the boy back. How old is he?'

'Sixteen.'

'Sixteen.' Ebla thought, 'Is he sixteen or eighteen?'

'And he has never been to school?'

'No. And never will.'

'But how could you send him back. Why this punishment?'

'It is not punishment. I want him to learn his trade, and he is happy.'

'You know how you were created?' he asked smiling.

'Yes, from clay like you,' she replied, also smiling.

'Not from clay! Adam was created by God from clay. I mean from where woman was created.'

'Yes, I know,' Ebla said.

'But don't tell me. Let me tell you.'

'Why should you tell me? I know it. I know where woman was created from.'

'But don't tell me. Let me tell you that they were created from the crooked rib of Adam.' After saying this, Awill kept silent for a while. Then Ebla, who had been also talking and not listening to him, added, 'And if anyone tries to straighten it, he will have to break it.'

Although the sun was not down, the room was quite dark.

'Should I tell you everything, Awill?' Ebla asked after a long silence.

'Maybe tomorrow when you have thoroughly decided,' he said. Awill closed the door, went and took a bath and then came back. Both naked, they got under the same cover and Ebla wondered if tomorrow's sun would rise with happiness, and the morning brightness would bring along some encouragement. She also wondered if she would tell him everything she had done during his absence.

'Tomorrow,' said Awill, moving towards her with desire.

'Tomorrow. We will tell each other everything tomorrow. You'll tell me everything, and I shall tell you everything.'

Ebla smelt his maleness. She touched his forehead and, as usual, he was hot with desire. He smiled at her and she smiled back at him.

'Poor fellow, he needs me,' she thought. 'He is sex-starved.'

'Yes. Tomorrow,' Ebla murmured and welcomed his hot and warm world into her cool and calm kingdom.

CHANDIGARH (INDIA)

19th March – 15th April, 1968.

GLOSSARY OF SOME SOMALI WORDS

Nabad Peace be unto you. '*Salam*' is the Arabic equivalent for *Nabad* which is also in common use among the Somalis.

Hamar Local name for Mogadiscio.

Harr Roughly noon-time.

Qora Breakfast.

Qado Lunch.

Sholongo This is some form of savings account common among women before the advent of banking in Somaliland. Each woman pays a specific amount daily, which can be withdrawn only when one's turn comes.

Ashantu This is a bastard form of the Arabic word *Ahsanta*, which means 'thank you'. *Mahadsanid* is the Somali equivalent; it has been coined recently, and isn't as often used as the former.

Yarad The price paid to the parents of the bride or her relations by the bridegroom and/or his relations.

Meherr A token amount either in kind or cash paid to the wife in case of divorce or death of husband. Naming of the amount is considered an important factor of the marriage contract. But it is more or less a promise the husband makes to the wife or her relations before they embark on the marriage: this is done in the presence of witnesses.

Wilaya This is the acceptance-of-the-marriage-to-Mr-So-and-So word uttered by the bride or her relations. Since the bride is never present at the engagement spot, she entrusts the word to a male member of her relations or a man of God who speak on her behalf.

Adan and Hawa The Somali equivalent of Adam and Eve.

Waji Fur This literally means 'Opening of the Face', and is common in the South of Somalia and the Somali part in Ethiopia. Being for the first time the bridegroom meets the bride, the fee is paid to the bride on the opening of her face.

Khaddar This is supposed to be the prophet of Mercy.

Fal Foretelling the future by drawing dots on the ground.

Amhar A member of the dominant Ethiopian tribe.